"[A] tour-de-force of cosmic weirdness, full of imagination and verve, that will leave you both bewildered and hungry for more. Winter is an exciting new talent in horror and once you cut into *The Guts of Myth*, you won't be able to put it down until the last strange bite."

—Evelyn Freeling, author and editor

PRAISE FOR "THE MOURNER ACROSS THE FLAMES" by SCOTT J. MOSES

"Once again Scott J. Moses has decided to rip out my heart, pummel it with grief, and leave it desiccated like a cheap valentine blowing in the wind across a nuclear wasteland. What a glorious story."

—Joe Koch, author of *The Wingspan of Severed Hands*

"By the end of the first chapter, I could taste salt, feel salt on my fingers, even hear the salt. Profoundly strange and unsettling from the start, the surreal setting serves as a perfect vehicle by which to deliver these profoundly human emotions and profoundly human pains, in a world where you never feel safe and hardly ever feel human. I am left feeling not only touched, but scrubbed raw, inside and out, in the most satisfying way."

—Alex Woodroe, editor at Tenebrous Press

"Scott J. Moses blends the emotional turmoil of loss, grief, and a desperate search for meaning after the unthinkable occurs, with as sure a talent as he does when bringing together dark fantasy, horror, and the post-apocalyptic narrative. Impossible to classify, this unforgettable novelette showcases Moses's uncanny skill at creating grand, awe-inspiring otherworld landscapes populated with complex characters who come alive in the moral gray areas."

—Patrick Barb, author of *The Nut House* and *Gargantuana's Ghost*

"Moses delivers a hallucinatory spiral of emotive horror that stuck to me like radiation."

—Eric Raglin, author of *Nightmare Yearnings*

SPLIT SCREAM

VOLUME ONE

Featuring:

CARSON WINTER

&

SCOTT J. MOSES

SPLIT SCREAM
Volume One

© 2022 by Dread Stone Press

Cover illustrations by Evangeline Gallagher
Interior illustrations by Marisa Bruno
Cover & interior design by Dreadful Designs
The Guts of Myth © 2022 by Carson Winter
The Mourner Across the Flames © 2022 by Scott J. Moses

Dread Stone Press
dreadstonepress.com

First Edition: September 2022

ISBN: 978-1-7379740-2-4 / Paperback Edition
ISBN: 978-1-7379740-3-1/ eBook Edition

For the love of horror, and all you weird ones.

INTRODUCTION

T he novelette has been dismissed and disparaged. Some dictionaries don't even define them as a unique form, listing only short stories, novellas, or novels. Others write them off as being "too sentimental" or "trivial".

This is silly, of course, and, with little effort it's easy to see the novelette has a purpose and value.

What makes a novelette, then? Exact word counts vary, but these stories are longer than a short story and shorter than a novella. Entertainment consumable in about an hour or two.

Sound like another form of easily digestible entertainment?

I'm not saying a novelette is a movie is a novelette. And I'm not saying written fiction *needs* to be like movies. But... But they are *kind of* like movies, right? If you're willing to accept that premise, at least for the moment, may I present to you...

SPLIT SCREAM
A Novelette Double Feature

Truly, what better way to present these stories than as a double feature? Do you *have* to read them back to back in a single Friday night after dusk? Certainly not. But could you? Absolutely.

So, what do you say?

You'll first bop along the twisted, quippy world of Carson Winter's "The Guts of Myth." Haven't you always wanted weird, cosmic, hardboiled noir? Sure you have. Then, slow it down with a trip to the barren salt flats, imbued with grief and delusion in Scott J. Moses's "The Mourner Across the Flames." There's a thread of love there, too, that you'd be remiss to let go.

Well, are you ready? Grab some popcorn, turn the lights low, and don't be afraid to scream.

This is but Volume One of the *Split Scream* series. I do hope you enjoy, and that you come back for more.

Long live the novelette!

Alex Ebenstein
Dread Stone Press
Michigan, USA
July 2022

CONTENTS

THE GUTS OF MYTH

Carson Winter

1.

I always thought I looked a little like Roger Moore. I wore the same suits and I had the same chestnut hair. We were both English, even though I only got in on a technicality. The real difference between us was that he was a movie star and I was a crook. But that was fine. I doubted either of us were keeping score.

London was alive with shit and smog. Double-decker buses and mean-faced bastards like myself ruled the streets—guys with bruised knuckles, red eyes, and a lust for carnage. It was a scary place, I guess—at least for everyone else. But it was 1973 and I was loving every minute of it. Because, you see, everyone else grew up here. They watched it change, or worse, they didn't watch it at all. I was an Anglophile—a perversion born of spending most of my youth in the States. In Seattle, of all places. That's why I didn't sound like Roger Moore, but holy shit did I want to.

When I was going around London saying shit like *lad* and *mate*, no one bothered correcting me. I couldn't help my flat accent, just like I couldn't help how my face looked cut up and vicious. I wasn't a big guy, everyone could see

5

that. But they could tell I was mean. They could see that I was willing to go a lot further than the other guy.

That's why I was at Mikey's, this old hole-in-the-wall pub that still played Sinatra while old-timers smoked. The lights always flickered there, and I could swear there was always some middle-class geriatric nodding off in a corner. In the back of the building was a little room where some local hoods—lads like me—did business.

Clarence nodded at me when I walked in and told me to take a seat. He wasn't a particularly nice guy, but he was efficient. Gaunt, widow's peak, cheekbones you could cut metal on. He had blue eyes, and if they were on a warmer looking guy, you might even say he was handsome. But, for me, he was a total no-go. You had to be careful going after guys like Clarence. Everyone's fine with a little buggery until they get caught doing it, and then suddenly the pitch-forks are drawn and you're bleeding out somewhere in the Thames.

"Good morning, Byron."

"Is it?"

"When you come to me and you give me money, then yes, it is a fine morning. Let's have it."

Clarence's eyes were like ice. You couldn't small talk that guy worth a damn. I pulled out a wad of pounds and handed them to him all nice like. He didn't like it when you threw money on his desk. Everything had to be placed in his hands. He was fussy like that.

He counted it and nodded. "Very well."

"I heard you had something for me today."

Clarence looked at me as if he had no clue what I was saying. He reached out for a cigarette, lit it, and puffed it for a couple seconds, not speaking until after he blew out a cloud of smoke. We all worked on Clarence's clock and he knew it.

"Yes, of course. There's a gentleman who approached me the other day. He was looking for a common thug. I told him I knew several."

"You're not shy about your associations, are you?"

"Never. But I've worked hard enough that I don't have to be coy. I'm not sure I know your excuse."

"American brashness, I suppose. Do you know who this guy is?"

"I don't. But he knew where to find me so he's worth knowing. He left a card for whoever wanted to talk. I figured you'd be as good as any other."

"How much does it pay?"

"I haven't a clue."

"Why not?"

"Because he wasn't asking me to take part. He was asking me if I knew anyone. I told him I did and I'd pass the message along. My part is done."

He handed me the card.

"Dr. Paul Gossam," I read.

"The address is on the back."

"I know where this is. But it's not a place a doctor lives."

"Indeed."

"What'd this cunt look like?"

He winced at my language. "A normal fellow. Well-dressed, but not showy. His shoes were Italian, I knew that. Well-bred, carefully spoken. Maybe about fifty-years old."

"And you don't know anything about what he wants from me?"

"Not a clue."

"Strange."

Clarence took a long drag of his cigarette. "It's not uncommon for a man to practice discretion in his affairs."

"Sure, sure," I said. The way Clarence looked at me, and the way he talked—that discretion shit—it was that sort of thing that made me want to make good on those blue eyes and ask him straight out how he swung. But I had a feeling the moment I asked would be the moment I signed a bullet into the back of my head.

"Is that all?"

I took the hint and left Clarence behind me. He breathed a long dragon's breath of smoke as I passed through the doors and out into the streets, with Dr. Gossam's card in my hands.

An hour later.

I couldn't understand what the guy on the street was saying.

I say I'm British, but I'm British in the way Americans say they're Irish. I was born here, ostensibly, but years six to eighteen were spent in the States. I spent so much time being special for having been born across the ocean, the Union Jack became a part of my identity that was hard to shake. When I was a young man, I got into some trouble and had to leave stateside. Long story.

Over in Seattle, I was British enough for any red-blooded American boy and girl, but over here, it wasn't as easy. Over here, I was a yank and my accent was a painful mish-mash of forced slang and mixed pronunciation. Americans said I sounded British, Brits said I sounded American. I couldn't win.

So, it was no surprise I couldn't understand this old fucker who probably came from somewhere up North. He was telling me something important, but it just sounded like a posh goat braying at me. Then again—everyone here sounded posh to me.

This guy was trying to sell me something and I was trying to ask him for directions. We were speaking two different languages. If he wasn't as old as the colonies themselves, I might have bashed his fucking face in, but eventually he gave me something I could use—he pointed.

I followed his old gnarled finger and saw a set of industrial looking buildings with thick smoke pouring out of tall, ominous smokestacks.

I ducked down the pavement and into an alley, where I crossed over into a labyrinth of connected brick warrens. My Dr. Gossam practiced between a factory and a shipyard. I imagined his patients would have to step over broken glass and rusted iron just to shake his hand. I was beginning to suspect he wasn't the sort of doctor I imagined.

Men screamed at each other over the sound of machinery. I'd spent a lot of time in places like this in my line of work. Pushing speed to tired working class folks, or beating the shit out of low-lifes who owed too much, too fast. I liked to say I broke teeth for a living.

The door was slender and red and carved into the side of a copper green warehouse. I had to climb a flight of stairs that twisted around the outside of the building like a snake. There were numbers on the door that matched the card, so I knocked. Somewhere, much too close, kids were smashing glass bottles and laughing.

I waited.

The smashing continued, and I wondered if this were a ruse. Maybe Clarence was pulling my leg. Maybe he saw the flicker in my eyes when I looked at him and he wanted to put me in the grave before even a whiff of poofery wafted from my cock. I tapped my toe against the metal platform beneath my feet.

The sounds of industrial London overtook me. I could hear everything for a five-mile radius. The street kids breaking glass, couples screaming, honking horns, and just as I was about to get lost in it all, I heard footsteps approaching the door, hand in hand with the inevitable.

2.

D r. Gossam looked pretty much exactly as Clarence described him. He was fifty-something, well-bred, with a close-trimmed beard. He looked strong for his age. His hair was white, but he didn't look older because of it. He looked like the sort of fellow that swam in cold rivers and boasted of invigoration. We shook hands and he welcomed me in, leading me deep into a disaster.

"Excuse the mess. Byron, you said?"

"That's right."

"Named for the poet?"

"My parents were capital-R Romantics."

"Ah, I see. Lovely people, I'm sure."

The office was strewn with plaster and trash. The walls were concrete and covered in divots, crumbling in places. Most of the windows were frosted, diffusing cold gray light across the detritus. He took me through four different rooms until we reached the last, tucked into the back of the building. A desk and a chair sat in isolation. He motioned me toward the latter as he took his place behind the desk and smiled, surrounded by rubbish.

"Excuse the mess," he said again. "But I like to do my business in places I can trust."

"No wandering ears, I suppose."

"Correct. Can we agree to keep this conversation between the two of us?"

"Of course," I said, nodding. "What can I do for you, Dr. Gossam?"

He leaned back in his chair and steepled his fingers. "Do you know much about books, Byron?"

"A little. I've read one or two." I didn't tell him that my old man was a bookseller back in the States. I'd bound more books than any fifteen-year-old in the world at the time.

"Well, that's where this all begins, you could say. A book. A special book."

It started to come together—a paranoid, old, upper-class snob needed a man on the street to steal a book for his family's collection. "Do tell," I said.

"I think I'll have to tell you a story first, if you don't mind. I'll pay you for your time, of course."

This was shaping up to be better than I thought. "Go ahead. I don't mind at all."

And that's when things got weird.

3.

He held up a book, a small black book that looked brand new, hot off the press. "Have you ever heard of a man named Allosaurus D'Ambrosere?"

I would've laughed if his face hadn't been so stony.

Apparently, he knew that. He sighed heavily. "Yes, it's an absurd name. His friends called him Al, which helped mitigate the ribbing. He was an adventurer of sorts, an active intellectual you might say. His father was a paleontologist who discovered the bones of an Allosaurus—that's a dinosaur, old boy—somewhere in Utah on the very same weekend his son was born. Hence, the name. Al divided his time between New York, London, Paris, Beirut, Hong Kong, Tokyo and who knows where else. Allosaurus D'Ambrosere was a strange man with strange tastes, and I met him for the first time a decade ago.

"You see, it all started at a party. This was in 1964, when my late wife and I still went to galas and other such nonsense. I was invited by a friend who had a tenuous connection to the host. That is not to say that this was the sort of affair I was accustomed to, however. Indeed, to my tastes back then, it was an abomination. There were many times I clutched my wife and whispered to her, 'Now! Let's go,' before seeing another horrible sight that kept us entranced for a moment longer. There was performative sodomy, ritual sacrifice, and a litany of blasphemous behavior. The host, who I saw very little of at first, was a plump man with a sharp goatee and arched eyebrows. His hair was black with just the beginnings of gray. He was tall and sturdy looking and spoke with a cultured American accent—I had the immediate impression that he was the product of private schooling and money. Throughout the night, my wife and I boiled in just the sort of discomfort I'm sure he wished to inflict on us. I don't know why we stayed, except perhaps to see where it ended. We walked from room to room to see people in the throes of coitus and violence and sometimes both at the same time. We saw men and women couple with animals. We witnessed Satanic rituals performed by men in masks.

"As the night continued, my wife and I found the onslaught of taboo somewhat dull, tiresome even. We decided to leave. But as soon as we turned toward the door, a hand grabbed my shoulder. 'Not leaving so soon?' said a servant, his mouth wriggling into the wickedest of grins. He said, 'Come now, upstairs. Al would like to see you.'

"It was very strange for us but we came from an unbearably polite generation. So, we went with the man who took us to a great mahogany door, and behind it sat Allosaurus D'Ambrosere. My wife clenched my hand as we approached this smiling giant. He offered us a chair and closed his eyes for a long while then asked us who we were. He asked if we were interlopers, all in good spirits. He never seemed angry at all. We told him the truth, that a friend had invited us. He nodded and asked us how we liked his party. Again, we were truthful. I told him it was not to our taste, that we were humble Christians and didn't agree with the decadence before us.

"'Ah,' he said. 'Of course, my apologies. Perhaps you and your lovely wife would be keen to take a walk with me outside and I can tell you more about my little society here.'

"Macy and I looked to each other and considered the offer out of strained politeness. So, we followed Mr. D'Ambrosere outside and he told us about his travels. It turned out, he had much the same wanderlust as his father had, and he had the same passion for antiquity. He was a collector of sorts, not just of artifacts, but of ideas. He said that the party we attended was but an infantile display of that same curiosity. On our walk, he came across as humble, good-humored, and spirited. My wife seemed to enjoy him as much as I did. An hour before, our stomachs were turning and now we were in rapt admiration of this charismatic man with the large home and interesting friends. We smoked cigars and he invited us to return, under more conservative circumstances. We left a little later, feeling that the night had not been such a waste at all.

"Over the coming months, Al became a good friend of mine. We met weekly and I became intertwined with his affairs. He taught Macy and myself about polyamory. Are you aware of this? It's free love, just like all the young people in San Francisco were doing. Carnal love without attachments. Soon, we were engaging in orgies and smoking hashish. All in a couple months. It was an incredible time of my life, although now it is far gone away. I owe that to Al. He opened our minds to a lot of things. And he did so with kindness and encouragement.

"Al had a business on the side. He was a rare book buyer and he had slowly involved me in his dealings. I had an interest in books but had no real collection—not like his, anyway. Years later, I had a hand in much of his business affairs, running them on the side while he traveled. It was not unusual for him to call me excitedly about a new find, or some strange white whale of his that he was so very close to spearing. But, in 1969, something different happened. He traveled to the West coast of the United States, I know that, and he remained there for two years. For those two years, my wife and I mourned his absence. But of course, we also moved on. We grew older and quieter—although Macy grew much quieter than I, passing away soon after—and I continued to handle his business affairs.

"It was an evening in 1971 when I first heard from him again. The phone rang in the middle of the night and I knew instantly who it was. I answered, almost too eagerly, and there he was, my friend Al. He sounded tired, hoarse. 'Hello, old friend,' he said. 'I'm afraid things have gotten very bad for me. Very bad indeed. You and I will have to play a game now. A children's game. Hide and seek. I will hide—vanish, more like—and you will need to seek me out. Or rather, save me. Please, save me.' He said that, he really did."

Dr. Gossam paused and held up the little black book. "I received this in the mail two days later. A box of twenty with instructions to sell them. The little note inside the box was the last communication I ever had with Allosaurus D'Ambrosere. I did as instructed, with one deviation—I bought a copy for myself."

I wasn't sure what to make of any of this. "And?"

Dr. Gossam shrugged. "He has vanished, just as he said. For the last two years, I've carried out my investigation. If my friend is still alive, I want him back."

"He's been kidnapped?"

"In a manner of speaking." He paused, filling his pipe. "Do you believe in Hell?"

"No."

"You won't have to for this, but it'll help." He struck a match and soon the room smelled of fine tobacco. "Hell isn't a fair description of where Al is currently, but it is as close as our imaginations can get."

I was starting to get weirded out by this. "What do you want me to do then?"

"Go where I tell you and follow my instructions. Come back with Allosaurus D'Ambrosere."

18

I stared at what he held in his hands. "So, what about the book?"

He smiled. "Yes," he said. "The book."

4.

The warehouse room with the broken glass and crushed drywall was cold and quiet. I could see why the good doctor preferred it as a meeting place. But a part of me hoped that he didn't meet people here often. The idea of him holed up here all week bothered the shit out of me. It gave me the creeps. The thought of the upper crust commingling in places like *this* dragged my fantasies through the mud.

Dr. Gossam held the book up and flipped through it. "This is *The Damned Abattoir*. Al discovered it in the States."

"Discovered. Can a book be discovered?"

"This one can. I've requested information on it from a number of other booksellers and none of them knew about it. At least not yet."

"Who's the author?"

"Unknown."

"Did Al write it as a gag?"

"I considered that," said Dr. Gossam. "But reading it, it doesn't sound like Al at all. It's much more distinctively... *American*. No offense, of course. It's just not the sort of work one would associate with Al, who wrote floridly in his letters. *The Damned Abattoir* is a much more, how do I say, feverish work. It's written in a first-person style reminiscent of authors like Burroughs and Salinger. It is at times cryptic, surreal, and nightmarish."

"And you think the book has something to do with his disappearance? That D'Ambrosere discovered the book and then was on the run because of it?"

"Perhaps. But I won't know for sure until we find him. That being said, the book does have clues. Or at least, it gave me a handful of starting points."

"What starting points are these?"

He waved the question away. "You won't want to know. But even if you did, you wouldn't understand. Let's say this though: I have made a series of exact calculations following astral patterns based on my findings, and if you follow them precisely, you will be able to find my friend."

"What the fuck does that even mean?"

Dr. Gossam thought for a moment, scratching his goatee. "It means that I am a crack-pot. It means that I am Prometheus and I am playing with dangerous, dangerous fire. It also means nothing to you, and it shouldn't. Your job is to find D'Ambrosere and bring him back. This is a job you will be paid handsomely for. Can you do that?"

"How much is handsomely?"

He told me.

Real fucking handsome.

I blinked and I saw a silver Aston Martin, a flat in Soho. Fucking speech lessons so I could disappear behind a facade of posh cuntiness. "Okay. I'm still here. Where do I find him?"

"In one month exactly, you'll need to be in Hong Kong. I will give you directions from there. I have people working there that will assist you."

"You think D'Ambrosere is in China?"

Dr. Gossam shook his head. "No," he said. "But the portal is."

"The portal?"

He nodded slowly, savoring my confusion. "Byron, I am willing to pay you *handsomely* to go where no man has gone before. Or rather, one man before you. All I'm asking is for your willingness and blind belief. It'll do neither of us any good if you leave here with nothing but a good story and a couple hundred pounds for your time. If you must doubt what I have to say, fine. But for this plan to work, you must follow my instructions exactly. Is this something you can do?"

I imagined a future where I might be sitting, smoking cigars, and drinking brandy with a lot of old money chaps like that. So, I tried to fit the part. I tried to sound like him. "Why yes, old boy, I believe I can."

He smiled. "I have two partners picked out for you."

"I don't need no partners."

"You do if I say you do. It's essential you have two partners."

"Why is that?"

"Consider it a part of my calculations."

5.

A t home, I smoked and read and drank and day-dreamed about black books.

When I slept, I dreamt of rich-guy orgies—old wrinkled flesh slapping against sagging buttocks. Graying pubes being feasted upon by toothless mouths. I woke with a sizable erection I refused to touch.

Clarence called and told me my partners had arrived. I rubbed my eyes and got out of bed on shaky legs.

Outside, I strutted about looking my best. I had two names, a Timothy Tomlin and a Wilhelmina Dottir. Clarence gave them to me as if they were the names of horses, with a little commentary of his own. "They're nobodies, of course. But most likely serviceable if you need discrete and capable *thieves*." He said the last word as if he were mocking me, but I didn't know why. Clarence liked to pretend we both weren't working for the same people—*bad people.*

I was back at Mikey's in no time, hanging around one of the pool rooms in the back. Before long, I saw Clarence walk past me like he had a grandfather clock shoved up his ass. He grimaced and said, "Your friends are here."

"Thanks," I said. "How's the morning treating you?"

Clarence shook his head and left without answering. Typical.

Just as promised, a man and a woman arrived. Both were about the same age, late-twenties with that working-class hunger fixed in their eyes.

"I 'ear you're workin' with us," said the woman, Wilhelmina. I was expecting a German accent, but she sounded Cockney to my ears.

The big fella stared me down. "Little fucker, ain't ye?"

I looked between the two of them. The man named Tomlin was a foot taller than me with blond hair combed neatly to the side. His cut, however, was very far from neat. He looked poor as dirt. I assumed his mother or girlfriend still cut his hair. Wilhelmina was also a little taller than me, but not so much I felt threatened. She had auburn hair tucked under a beanie and a large winter coat that made her look much wider than she was.

"Right. Have you been told the details?"

Tomlin sneered. "Why don't you tell us?"

I told them the basics, that we'd be going to Hong Kong in one month to find a man with an absurd name. I left out all the occult bullshit. I did, however, tell them their cut.

"Just to take a trip? Fucking hell. We're in your service."

I picked up on Tomlin's continued use of 'we.' "Are you two a couple?" I asked.

They laughed at me and I thought I could probably take the two of them easily enough, but I let it slide. "We haven't shagged if that's what you mean," said Wilhelmina. "But we have worked together on occasion."

They laughed more at this and I balled my fists. "Are you going to tell me or are you gonna keep laughing?"

And then I heard Clarence, his crystalline voice cutting through their laughter. "He sells her. Or used to. As you Americans say, he's a pimp. And she's a whore."

I turned behind me, a look of surprise on my face.

"Gossam only hires the best," he said with a thin smile. He left the room as silently as he came.

The two others stood there nonplussed. I expected some outrage from them, but they took his comment as purely benign.

"Do either of you have experience in crimes beside prostitution?"

"I don't fuck for money anymore," said Wilhelmina. "We hunt bigger game now."

"That's right," said Tomlin. "We work in the arts."

"Paintings," she added.

"Cat burglars."

"You could say," said Tomlin. "We've done well for ourselves. For that price, I figure we could steal just about anything."

"Even a person?"

"Sure," said Tomlin. "Why not?" He sat down at the pool table, self-consciously rubbing his wrists, back and forth, like a nervous tic. I wasn't sure if I'd lost them or if they were deep in thought.

"The man's really named after a dinosaur, isn't he?"

"Afraid so."

Wilhelmina cackled at that, but the way they looked at each other, I thought she was laughing at me.

6.

If it'd been my choice, I would've taken that month to prepare, but there was nothing to do. We didn't know enough to do anything. I met with Dr. Gossam once more, but I was hurried out after ten minutes. He gave me my money and told me all would become clear when we reached Hong Kong. The only thing of interest he told me was this, on my way out. "Whatever happens, you must not hesitate. I need a man with a strong stomach."

I nodded quickly and was pushed out the door.

For the next month, the Art Dealers and I drank and smoked and talked. Wilhelmina revealed herself to be surprisingly sober, only drinking club soda when we all got together. "Can't risk alcohol," she said. "Too many bad experiences."

Tomlin, on the other hand, drank extravagantly. He poured spirits down his gullet and filled himself to the brim, so much so that I could swear the brown liquor was oozing out of his amber eyes. He was a handsome bloke and I considered the fact that I shouldn't be thinking that at all. So, I never said anything, but I did ask him how he started working with Wilhelmina.

"Grew up on the same block," he said, taking a drink. "She had something to sell and she needed protection.

Always liked Wilhelmina, I did. Wasn't no stretch to go into business together."

"Gets tiring after all. Sucking pricks, that is."

"And yet you were one of the best," said Tomlin seriously.

"Why'd you retire?"

Wilhelmina rolled her eyes up to the ceiling, blowing air through the corner of her mouth. "I used to 'ave this friend named Mary. Mary was your average London tart and she made about the same money as I did, but was about half as pretty. I honestly didn't know how she did it. We used to joke that she had a vibrating cunt. But then she started buying fur coats and cars and I knew something was up. I knew something was entirely wrong, because there's no way even a well-paid whore can afford fur coats and cars. We're only human. We'd 'ave to 'ave a line out the door, bunch of bastards working their pricks in queue, day to night. So, I went up and asked her one night and she told she wasn't whoring no more. In fact, she said she wouldn't ever do it again. I asked her, 'how?' because honestly, no whore likes being a whore. You don't choose it as a vocation. No little girl tells her Sunday school teacher that she wants to get fucked by a thousand men who 'ate her for a living. So, I was all ears. Mary said to me, 'I'm not whoring no more, I'm killing.' She was a dumb slag for telling me that. But it gave me some ideas. The next three that Timmy brought to me, I slit their throats in their bed and emptied their wallets, all without touchin' they pricks."

"Furious, I was," said Tomlin. "I didn't know."

I took a drink. I wasn't one to judge.

"Aye, that's true. Tomlin 'ad no idea. When he found out, I thought he was going to beat the Jesus into me, but he saw I'd been 'iding the bodies in my closet and they were beginning to stink. I couldn't move them much further than that."

"So, I come up there and after stomping around for a bit, I tell her we can't ever do anything like this again, too dangerous. Then, I helped her get rid of the bodies."

"How'd you get them out?" I asked, genuinely curious.

Wilhelmina laughed. I could tell she admired Tomlin. "He brought up a saw and we got to cutting those stiff pricks into pieces. For the next three days, we went in and out of the apartment, taking a body part at a time covered in plastic in our satchel. We dumped them in the river, in sewers, some of them we burned. Neighbors must've thought we were forgetful, going back and forth all the time, but I figured they were used to the comings and goings at my flat."

"After that," said Tomlin, "I told her we needed a new job. Couldn't very well go around and kill every john in London, could we? Although I'm sure Wil would've been up to the task. After that, I read an article about the theft of a painting that was worth a million dollars. Can you imagine that? A fucking painting. Colors on canvas. Bloody ridiculous. Anyways, that turned some gears in my head and I started going to museums. Wearing my best suits, making friends with those in the scene. I wasn't stealing anything yet, but it was research all the same. I started bringing Wil with me so they wouldn't think I was queer. We started by swiping books, just for research. To read. We went to the library too. We're quick studies, we are. You wouldn't know it, but we're smarter than we look. What you don't know about these old fuckers is that every single one of them would kill to have an original Rembrandt, and not a single one of them gives a shit how."

I let out a yawn. "Quite the tale," I said, warm beer sloshing in my stomach.

His eyes narrowed. "So, what is it that got you into this operation?"

"Haven't a clue."

"What do you fucking do?"

"Act mean, break teeth."

"That it then?" He laughed. "They cut a little yank fucker like you in, for no fucking reason whatsoever?"

"That's it. But I'm not a yank," I tried to explain. "I mean, I lived there, but I was born here."

Wilhelmina rolled her eyes. "Sounds like a yank to me."

"The accent got bullied out of me, I'm afraid."

Tomlin stood up. He towered over me. "Are you sure you want to go through with this?"

I nodded toward the back of the house. "Clarence recommended me."

"And why would he do that? You been buggering each other back there?"

Wilhelmina cackled like a hyena.

"I used to do a lot of work for him," I said. My lips spread, I showed my teeth.

"Little fella like you? Little Napoleon or something? What happens if I beat you to death right here in this bar?"

I shrugged. "You won't. You can't."

"That a challenge?"

Wilhelmina squealed. How easily these friends turned against me. I'd have to talk to Clarence about that later. But I knew exactly what he'd say. *Oh, did your ruffians not respect you? Did you do anything to earn their respect?*

I had come to find that violence was the only thing that triumphed over class.

I stood up. I didn't bother puffing out my chest because I didn't have the taste for theatrics that went into fighting. I did give him an out though. "We're gonna be working together soon. We're gonna be stuck with one another. Are you gonna want to work with me if I crack your skull across the table?"

The bartender, bored, said, "Go on then, take it outside."

Tomlin was out the door. He was drunk, whether he knew it or not. And I was behind him, six steps, then two. In another, I was in front of him and he didn't know I could be that fast, that sure-footed. But I was. I boxed all my years in the states. I knew the footwork.

But he was tall and had a reach and he thought that was going to be enough. So, I stood there and began considering backups to our Chinese excursion. I didn't know if this was Gossam's man or Clarence's—but I was sure there were a lot like him. The air was crisp and cold and smelled of smoke and booze. It smelled like my city, my birthright.

"You're gonna give me your cut when I beat the piss outta you, right?"

"Right," I said. "And when you're sobbing on the concrete, I'm gonna take one of your teeth. My choice."

Wilhelmina leaned against a pillar. The street was empty except for the three of us. Tomlin raised his arm and began to rock back and forth. I took a couple steps back and got ready for his hit.

He was quicker than I thought. He punched fast and if it'd hit me, I'd have been knocked out for sure. I had to admire blokes like Tomlin, naturally gifted. I let him swing a couple more times, weaving in and out of his sharp jabs like a hummingbird.

The bastard was sure he had me. So fucking sure.

I got him into a rhythm, and as soon as he was in it, I snapped my fist into his chin. He threw left, but I got in close and he couldn't do much but rub his bicep across my cheek. When my punch landed, I felt his head turn on a swivel.

He fell backwards a couple steps and shook his head. He growled. He got lower this time.

He wasn't expecting me to jump.

My feet slammed squarely into his head and for a vicious moment, my body was parallel to the ground. I think it was then he realized he'd made a mistake, because as he got up from the ground, stumbling and seeing stars no doubt, I thought I saw the beginnings of his hands going up. *Please, stop.* But that's when I flew toward him, pushing him to the ground, slamming the back of his head into the asphalt. I wasn't a spectacular fighter, not really. But I never had to be. I lost every match I ever fought in the States. And if Tomlin had me under regulation rules, the ref would have his fist up and the crowd would be cheering as I bled out through my nostrils on the ring floor. But it wasn't, because there was no ref, there was just Wilhelmina running toward me, telling me to stop. There was just Tomlin with his skull cracking against the pavement as I threw all my weight into it, lifting my knees up off the ground and driving it further into the street.

"What the fuck are you doing?" said Wilhelmina, apparently having enough of the scene.

"Fighting," I said.

Tomlin's eyes didn't open, but he was still conscious. Likely with a concussion. I breathed hot breath on his face and reached for my back pocket.

"The reason I'm here isn't because I'm bigger, friend," I said. "It's because I'm willing to go further. Open wide."

Before he knew what was happening, I had my wallet shoved into his mouth and my knees on either side of his head. He threw weak blows at my side but couldn't gain any momentum. When he opened his eyes, I noticed one pupil was larger than the other. One big black disc, one pinprick. He was probably seeing double.

"You can go to the hospital soon," I said. "But remember we had a wager."

In my jacket pocket was a small knife. Nothing fancy. But it didn't have to be to dig through the meat of his gums. I flicked it open and claimed my prize.

7.

D r. Gossam mailed me one letter before we left—an envelope stuffed with money and handwritten instructions for our landing. The whole time we were waiting to leave, Tomlin was looking at me out of the corner of his eye, tonguing the spot where I took his tooth.

After that night, things had changed. Wilhelmina and I hurried him to the hospital and they numbed him and checked him for a concussion. Wouldn't let the poor bastard sleep. He turned out okay though, although maybe a little less focused after. He seemed to go to a different place when he sat alone for too long, but he was a lot more demure. Subservient, even. They were afraid of me now and I liked that.

On the plane, we all smoked quietly. There was nothing to say, really. Tomlin's eye was still dilated, and would likely be for the rest of his life. I offered him a cigarette, which he took like a lobotomized servant shamefully accepting his master's grace. Wilhelmina wasn't much better. Her bitter laughter had been killed and she was rigid and purposeful. I liked them better this way, honestly.

Basically, I felt great.

When we landed in Hong Kong, I didn't really know what to think. I hadn't been to any place that didn't speak English before, so I shut down a little bit. We arrived at night and tasted factory smoke when we got out on the tarmac. The air was warm, and Tomlin and Wilhelmina didn't seem so impressed. But out there, somewhere, was a sprawling city and that made me anxious.

I pulled out Dr. Gossam's letter. "We're meeting an expat local, a friend of D'Ambrosere's. An American named Karkarr."

Tomlin opened his mouth to say something, then closed it.

I finished for him. "Funny name, I know. Lots of men with strange names."

Wilhelmina said, "We need a cab."

"Yes," I said. "We do. Call one, why don't you?"

Cars zipped by, Chinese lettering slashed along their sides in deep black. I felt uncomfortable at the fact that I was surrounded by so much language and yet understood none of it. When a car stopped, we squeezed into the back seat, Wilhelmina in the middle and Tomlin staring blankly out the window.

"Here," I said.

The driver didn't understand me at all but took my paper, furrowed his brow, then nodded. "Okay," he said, which I think was all the English he knew. And soon, we were weaving toward a city filled with light.

The other two sat frozen, but I tried to take it all in. We had work to do.

We all got out onto a bustling thoroughfare filled with street vendors. Just like in the movies. I'd watched a couple kung fu flicks to immerse myself in the culture, but it didn't do much except teach me how to fight with wires on your back. The food smelled delicious though.

I thought about getting a stick of meat or a bowl of soup but Dr. Gossam left strict instructions to find Karkarr immediately. There was no question to the urgency, as he underlined it many times: *ASAP*.

We walked down the long street of vendors and headed toward what looked like a slum. Trash was strewn on the street, drunks slept off a hard day's night next to garbage cans, tough looking kids with tattoos mean-mugged us walking by. In some ways, it was just like home.

"Up here," I said, reasonably sure I was heading the right way. The good doctor left us a map in the envelope he mailed me. "We're meeting with a chap named Ezekiel Karkarr."

"Does he have D'Ambrosere?"

I smiled because it was the first time Tomlin had spoken directly to me beyond one-word answers. Maybe his ego was healing after all.

"I don't think so," I said. "But I don't know either."

Wilhelmina sniffed the air. "Whatever this place is, I'm not sure I like it."

I pressed onward. "We don't have to like it, we just have to collect our checks."

Clarence, somewhere, was laughing. I think I knew exactly why he selected me for this job. He knew I was dogged, unfazed, stubborn. I was starting to believe in my own myth.

I think my partners did too, because they didn't dare look at me when I talked. That was good in my book. I felt confident, capable.

"This is it," I said. "This is Chez Karkarr."

We were standing before a stone townhouse with thin windows. It looked shabby, old. Lights were on inside and I could smell the faint scent of marijuana. I knocked on the door and heard them echo through the home. Inside, I heard a rustling.

Wilhelmina and Tomlin looked at each other. The moment we were sharing was of palpable anticipation. We'd traveled halfway around the world to find a man we'd never met, for money we could never imagine.

After a minute or so, the door opened and the weed scent became strong. A man in black goggles opened the door, his hair was long and wild and sticking out in spikes. He wore a red bathrobe, tied around the waste.

"And who are you three?"

"We are the three horsemen from the Calico Fair," I said, remembering my instructions.

The man took a step forward and looked both ways. "Nobody followed you?"

"Not that we know of."

"You don't look very inconspicuous."

"We couldn't if we tried."

"No one's followed us," Wilhelmina said. "I've been watching."

He nodded. "Alright then, come inside. Quick now."

He ushered us into an empty room. His home, if it were actually his, was rotting from the inside out. Dust coated every surface. The walls were a sickly dun, the color of a coffee stain. The place wasn't inhabitable by any good measure.

"It's the laboratory—that's what I call it. You can thank our mutual friend. You want a drink?"

"Yes, please," said Tomlin, whose great black eye shimmered under the webbed chandelier. He looked tired after the journey. But he was tired all the time now.

"Just a water," said Wilhelmina. She walked to the side of me, eyeing each corner of the room with suspicion.

"You, sir?"

"Gin, if you have it," I said.

Karkarr threw his head up and down so deeply that I almost thought he was bowing for a moment. "You've come here to party. I like it."

He disappeared from the room and Wilhelmina immediately grabbed me by the neck, pulling herself to my ear. He hadn't even been gone for a second before she said, "We can still leave."

Tomlin looked away, shaking his head.

"We need to leave," she said. "Or it's gonna be *bad*."

She let me go when she heard Karkarr's wobbling footsteps come back. The man walked with a strange gait, pigeon-toed or something. His feet were pointed at odd angles, always misaligned with his knees.

He brought us drinks. I sniffed. It was gin, alright.

"You're probably wondering why you're here," he began. "But that's not going to matter too much to you. Because 'why' isn't your concern. Your concern is lining your pockets and my concern is leading you to the gateway. That's where you'll find your man, by the way. Allosaurus D'Ambrosere."

"He's here then?"

"No. But you'll figure that out soon enough."

"Are you giving us any weapons?" asked Wilhelmina.

Karkarr had a beer of his own in his hand. "Sure, you can take a gun if you want. Fuck it, have this one." He reached into his robe and retrieved an automatic pistol. Tomlin had already started toward him, but Karkarr had his hand up: *please, wait, stop.* Tomlin, unlike I would have, actually halted.

40

He handed the gun to Wilhelmina. She weighed it in her hand. "This it, then? You're gonna give us a gun and say we're safe?"

"I never once said you're safe. In fact, I'll confirm you're not. You're paid well enough to not be safe in the least. How's that?"

Wilhelmina whipped her head around and whispered something in Tomlin's ear. By the look of his face, I could tell it wasn't anything good. I could take Tomlin, especially now that he was a walking, talking potato, but if they both decided to turn on me, I'd be shit out of luck. Wilhelmina had the gun and she could have me sleeping eternally in a dumpster if she liked. But Tomlin's mouth stayed a firm line and he shook his head, never looking at me. I'd have to talk to them. I'd have to keep them in line.

Karkarr said, "You three will start tonight. It's just up-stairs in fact. I'll explain how it works when we get up there. But you're not going to like it, I'll let you know that right now. For now, enjoy your drinks. In an hour, you'll be somewhere else."

"How?"

He put up a finger. "Just drink your gin. No more questions."

8.

"Are you two good?" I asked.

"We're bloody fantastic," she spat.

Karkarr was upstairs, preparing for us. He didn't say how or why, only that he was preparing.

"We've got a lot on the line here," I said. "If it wasn't us, it'd be three other nobodies. And they too would be shitting themselves. But I bet if we saw them coming back to London and living in a nice flat and not working for the rest of their goddamn lives, we'd have wished we did what they did. You both want to steal paintings for the rest of your days?"

"We'll be fine," said Tomlin. "You got anything besides hitting debtors?"

"I take *pride* in my work," I said. I was provoking him, but I couldn't help it. "But if I never had to throw another punch outside a boxing ring, I'd be a happy man. We could do *anything*. We'd never have to see each other again after this."

Wilhelmina shook her head. "I, for one, am not worried about seeing you again."

"Stop it," said Tomlin. He turned to her. "What do you make of the mad scientist?"

Wilhelmina opened her mouth to speak. "He's—"

"Karkarr's not going to bloody kill us," I said. "You have the fucking gun, what more do you want?"

"The gun won't solve anything," she said.

"It can solve one thing," said Tomlin.

Rage boiled within me. "It wasn't my idea to fight."

"You're a fucking wanker, you know that?"

"I can make sure you eat through a straw for the rest of your life."

Tomlin laughed, he squared up to me. "You fucking idiot. You think I've never gotten hit before? This isn't about that. How dense are you? Have you noticed the fucking walls?"

I turned to follow his gaze. "What the fuck is that?" I said.

The walls were covered in them, but they weren't painted—rather, they were *cleaned* into the walls. They were spread haphazardly—different sizes and shapes, covering the wall from floor to ceiling.

"Fucking runes or something," said Wilhelmina. "I can't make them out, of course. But they're runes, all the same."

Tomlin nodded. "You ever think about what always seems to follow strange runes and strange people?"

They looked at me expectantly.

"They need us to bring back their dinosaur."

"Right," said Tomlin. He seemed exasperated.

"The people we're working for are off," I conceded. "Dr. Gossam is an occultist. These people believe in magic. This is part of the package deal."

Wilhelmina shook her head. "You want to die for these people?"

Tomlin sighed, a chuckle escaping his lips. "He's made his mind up. We may as well follow our leader into the abyss."

They looked at each other and I could tell they were in quiet disagreement. But there was also something else.

Whatever they shared dissipated when Karkarr called to us. "Ready," he shouted.

They motioned for me to go first, with a hint of theatricality. My heart was beating too hard for questions. By the time I reached the top, by the time Karkarr opened the door, by the time we saw the man though, I was ready to run.

9.

The funny thing was, the runes were the first thing I saw. It was a small room with a tall ceiling, one lightbulb that cast yellow light and black shadows. The runes weren't cleaned into the wall here, I'm not even sure they were painted, they looked more like they'd been slashed. Wilhelmina and Tomlin had the same reaction as I did once the door closed behind them, an explosion of quiet adrenaline and locked knees.

We all saw the man at the same time.

He was a Chinese man, somewhere in his mid-thirties, if I had to guess. He shook his head violently back and forth, making inchoate noises from behind the dirty strip of fabric gagging his mouth. He was completely nude, tied tight to the chair he sat on.

"I'd introduce you," said Karkarr. "But I can't for the life of me pronounce his name. For the sake of this conversation, we're going to call him the Gateway, because that's exactly what he is."

"The Gateway," said Wilhelmina, as if she were familiarizing herself with the term.

"Or the portal, if you prefer."

"Who is he?"

Karkarr shrugged. "A victim of circumstance, of mathematics. Of being alive in the wrong time, in the wrong place. Dr. Gossam has no doubt told you of his calculations?"

"He mentioned them briefly."

"Well, now you can see them for yourself. This is where Dr. Gossam has led us, but only for a thirty-six-minute window."

There were too many questions. "But—but—"

"This is a lot to take in. We have five minutes before the portal is open. Let me explain, quickly."

"Alright," I said. "Do tell."

"The man you're looking for, as you've been told many times, is not in Hong Kong. But the portal to him is indeed in this fine city of filth. You're meeting the portal right now." He went around to the scared, shaking man and placed his hands on his shoulders. "Dr. Gossam located this man through a series of predictive calculations taken from *The Damned Abattoir* and the works of Mr. D'Ambrosere himself. We believe that Al is not on this earth anymore, but on a different plane of existence. An alternate reality, perhaps."

Karkarr held up his palms and placed them together. "Imagine this is the world you live in, then imagine you make a choice." He moved one hand away from the other. "Now, you have a whole other dimension where one day you chose to have coffee instead of tea, you dig? Well, consider this an alternate reality. Also, consider that this alternate reality might not even be an alternate to ours. It could be an alternate of an alternate of another, many, alternates. These are worlds we don't know. What we do know is that D'Ambrosere was very interested in these worlds. We are standing here, today, on the shoulders of giants."

The man in the chair, the Gateway, tried to scream.

"Tonight, you three will travel through this man to find Allosaurus D'Ambrosere and bring him back to our plane."

"This is fucking lunacy," said Tomlin.

Wilhelmina touched his hand. "I don't think it is."

I looked at the both of them like I was watching a play.

They turned to me for support, but I just shrugged. "I was told to go in ready to believe whatever dumb shit I was told. For the right price, I can do that."

They shook their heads. "This fucking prick."

"Careful," I said.

They had a plan, I knew it. They were holding grudges.

Karkarr was silent through this but was shaking his head.

"Let's not forget who's got the gun," said Wilhelmina, finger tickling the trigger.

"Trust me, I haven't forgotten. I'll have my fingers popping his eyes out before you can squeeze off a shot," I said, blood rushing to my face.

"The gateway will open soon!" screamed Karkarr.

We all shut up.

Wilhelmina stared me down with the barrel. Karkarr went to the man and said some words I couldn't understand. I had my hands up. I was all bluster.

"We all need to go in to get paid," I said, carefully. "Dr. Gossam made that very clear."

"Well, fuck off. I'm not going."

"Me fucking either."

But I knew that wasn't true. Because I could see their posture. They *were* going. They were going to go no matter what I said. Their mouths spat and cursed and threatened, but their lips and limbs betrayed a lackadaisical willingness. I shook my head. *I'm getting paranoid*, I thought.

Karkarr had pulled a knife and the man was screaming now. Karkarr turned to us and said, "Listen now, this gate isn't open forever, so when you come out, it'll be in a new one. Dr. Gossam didn't tell me where or when though. When you come out, you might be in fucking Argentina for all I know. But that's not my business. Dr. Gossam does the mathematical magic, I just follow instructions. Once I cut this fellow open, you're going to want to go in one at a time. Are you ready?"

"Fucking hell," said Tomlin, reading his lines.

"No fucking way," said Wilhelmina, back.

Karkarr stabbed through the man's sternum and dragged the knife down to his waist.

The dying man screamed through his gag and began to shake violently. The wound formed a stretch of red highway down his front that sent cascades of blood running down his genitals, pooling on the floor. His guts squirmed inside of him, the whiteness of his bones gleamed and when the man could not scream anymore, he bit. His teeth tore madly at the gag in his mouth, and I thought he might get through it for a second, but nothing happened. His teeth were impotent tools and the blood was running and Karkarr was yelling: "Quick! Quick! Get ready!"

The air left our lungs all at once.

The man was still shaking, but he was also *opening*. Wet cracks and bony pops emanated from his shifting form. His neck snapped to the side and everything that was inside him seemed to expand. A violet light, eerie and calm, began to shine from somewhere in his insides—which seemed deeper than any I'd ever seen before, now that I thought about it. Idly, I considered the thought: *how can a man be so deep?* I'd seen the insides of men many times before, and never—

His body was forced upward, still tied to the chair, but now he was continually growing. There was no new flesh, but it was as if all of the bones inside his body had reached a mutual decision to change their shape, to become an arch. And so now, they did. His head flattened at the top of the arch, blood and drool soaking through his gag, his eyes crushed and oozing viscous liquid down his compacted cheeks. He still quivered.

"Bloody fucking hell!" screamed Wilhelmina, facing the circular portal made of man in front of us. She was not acting now, I could tell.

Tomlin covered his eyes, heaving into the wall.

Karkarr pointed at me. "You first. Let's go. We don't have forever."

The tiny room with the black runes blew with cold gusts of sulfurous winds. I stared into the man's open middle, which, despite the shape his body had made, was not really so large at all. Really, it was just large enough for me to pass through, standing up—right into that liquid light.

"Go on now," said Karkarr. "We don't have time to stare at it!"

"Fuck this!" screamed Tomlin.

"No fucking way!" yelled Wilhelmina.

I took a step toward the light. I was feeling much the same way. The closer I stood to it, the more it made my insides shake. But, there was something alluring about it, I had to admit. I thought back to Dr. Gossam. And I saw a future for myself that I couldn't see without its gaping maw.

"We've got a job to do," I said.

And that's when Wilhelmina had the pistol aimed at my face.

I hated the whore, I realized. I wanted her to climb through that man's guts first. My hands stayed at my side. "If you want to shoot me, go on and do it."

Tomlin still had his head turned. He couldn't even stand to look at the thing. "Fuck off, ye cunt!"

I took a step toward her and she pulled the trigger three times fast.

Click. Click. Click.

I turned to Karkarr, who smiled. He held the magazine in his hands and then threw it into the portal—the man—where it disappeared.

That's when I lunged, grabbing her, pinning her arms to her side as she kicked and screamed. She was light and couldn't fight back, although she tried. My shoulder burned as her teeth dug into my flesh. I yelped, but I wasn't about to let her off.

I was at the man's gaping stomach when I heard Tomlin yell. "Don't you fucking dare!"

"Come and get her!" I screamed back.

Tomlin raced toward me, his one large black pupil reflecting the light from the man's middle like an oil slick. Just as his fingers grazed me, I fell backwards, into the light.

51

I let go of Wilhelmina and she vanished. I think I might have vanished as well. As I fell backward, I felt the wetness of cosmic guts—bone deep and frigid like silence. I saw Karkarr's smiling face at the top of the tunnel, staring down in wonder at our tumbling bodies.

In the space between Hong Kong and where we went, there was no sound but our natural rhythms—slamming hearts, circulating blood, and gasping lungs.

When we hit the ground, it felt as if we'd been sliding for hours. I had the strange sense of euphoria. Then I opened my eyes.

10.

W e were all there, all three of us, which I felt some pride in, honestly. I imagined telling Clarence or Dr. Gossam what had happened, how I had a mutiny on my hands, but with some quick thinking I had rallied my troops and ensured the mission would be successful. I was the right man for the job, after all.

Wilhelmina lay face down in scorched earth, a black sand that stretched forever. She lifted herself up, her eyes wide and lips quivering. She wanted to scream, "No," of course.

So did I. But there's a funny thing about fear—it's always easier to be courageous when someone else is more afraid. Seeing her fear made me feel better, stronger. Her eyes took in the vista in stunning disbelief.

Tomlin was lying face up, his larger pupil captured the image of the red sky above us. He shifted back and forth, like he was in agony, but I knew he wasn't. We didn't fall hard. Instead, it was as if we were gently dropped. More acting on his part.

I was the first one to stand. Ahead of us was a great cityscape. Towers touched the crimson sky, chunks missing from their structures. I marveled, because it didn't look so different from our own world, our own cities. But they had decayed violently. Vines and black vegetation grew over each of the abominable structures. We were outside of the city, perhaps only a quarter of a mile, and when I looked back at my compatriots, to see if they saw what I did, I realized they were both staring at something else entirely.

It blended in with the black sand almost too well. But when I saw it, I dived for it.

So did they.

Tomlin was on top of me, but Wilhelmina already had it in her hands. I threw a punch behind my head and managed to crack Tomlin good in his bad eye.

The whore was fumbling with the magazine.

I threw my weight into Tomlin and had him on his back, but he had me in a bear grip on his chest. Still, I was within reach. I kicked a foot out at Wilhelmina and sent the gun spiraling out of her hand.

She ran for it. I elbowed Tomlin one, two, three, four, five times in his kidney before he let me go and suddenly I was right behind Wilhelmina. She looked back at me in terror, in hate, and she once again had the gun.

She fitted the clip and slammed it back with one graceful movement. She raised it toward me.

But I was too close.

I had already reared back with my fist—I was wound up.

Tomlin yelled, "Stop!"

But I wouldn't, because if a half a second passed, I'd have a slug inside me and an exploding heart. So, my fist met her throat.

Her eyes bulged. I grabbed her wrist and twisted. The gun came out easily.

Wilhelmina stumbled away, holding her neck, coughing, trying to breathe and that's when I spun around to see Tomlin, running toward me.

"Stop it now or I'll kill both of you," I said.

Tomlin didn't stop, but he slowed. I jogged a little, to put distance between myself and the other two. It turned out, he didn't give a shit about me. He ran toward her.

"You 'right?" he asked her.

"Can't breathe," she choked.

"You can breathe," he said calmly. "Just do it slowly."

I had the gun trained on them as Tomlin gently patted her back and told her it was going to be okay. Above us, the sky went on forever.

"We've got to go to the city," I said. "It's in my notes. Dr. Gossam said we have to go to the city."

Both of them, in unison, looked up at me with eyes that could kill. But they wouldn't.

"If you want to go home, that's how it's going to happen," I said. "We can't leave now."

The thought scared me, but I knew they were more afraid than I was. I already fled one home, this was just another.

"I'm going to kill you," said Wilhelmina, hoarse. "I'm going to kill you."

"Alright. Save it for London."

"We're not going with you," said Tomlin, easily.

"You have no choice."

"We 'ave a bloody choice," he said.

I gestured to the city, to the sky, to the earth. "You have no choices here. We've got to do this together."

Somewhere, far away, the sound of agonized screeching. My stomach flipped. I held the gun with two hands.

"What was that?" said Wilhelmina.

"Natives," I said.

"No," said Tomlin.

"Let's move forward, get our money, and never see each other again. Sound good?"

The noises were followed by a great slithering, the sound of sand being displaced.

The two didn't say anything, but they followed me. Wilhelmina rubbing her throat, Tomlin with a hand at her back.

We walked toward the city, the great looming metropolis.

It looked familiar, somehow.

"Is it London?" I said.

Silence.

"It's a real city, right?"

Wilhelmina shook her head. "It's Beksinski, that's what it is."

"Who's that?"

"A painter."

"Untitled," said Tomlin. "We saw it in a gallery last year in Poland."

"It was a painting of this?"

Wilhelmina's lip curled in disdain. "No, it was a painting *like* this. Nightmarish. I don't think this city exists anywhere but here. If it does, I'd ask for you to shoot me now. And I'd make sure you didn't miss."

We continued on. I couldn't tell if this had been a civilization destroyed by nuclear war or if this decay was built into it for aesthetic considerations. The towers looked to be obsidian, and where they broke, they broke cleanly in shards. Inside of them, empty homes and offices were caked in a layer of dust and ash. I couldn't imagine someone, anyone, living here. I couldn't imagine them waking up in the morning and looking up at that blood red sky and calling this home.

Still, as we moved forward, there were noises coming from every which direction. It was not a quiet place, no matter how much we wished it to be. Wilhelmina, Tomlin, and I kept spinning, on eternal lookout.

"Where's he supposed to be anyways?"

"We came here for the wanker with the funny name, where the fuck is he?" asked Tomlin.

"Somewhere in the city, I guess." I couldn't help it. My voice betrayed my wonder. "He could be anywhere though. It's a big world."

"Don't say that," said Wilhelmina. "I don't want to hear that."

"Me neither. But here we are. It's beautiful though, isn't it?"

They didn't answer me.

We were on the streets now, in the city proper. They were paved, just like ours at home. Except these had been unattended so long that alien vegetation grew from their cracked surfaces. I held the gun like a talisman, no longer able to deny Dr. Gossam his occultist blabber. I was about as spiritual as a DMV, but here I was—on another plane.

Thinking about how I got here made me sick to my stomach. And then I thought of the poor bloke who had the dumb luck of having a predetermined portal stuck inside him. *Welp, bad luck.*

Tomlin stopped.

He was already pointing for Wilhelmina. "I see it," she said.

"What do you see?"

They looked to each other as if they still had to decide whether I deserved to know anything. Finally, it was Wilhelmina who said, "Look, over there."

I took a step forward and they dropped back. *Cowards,* I thought. *I'm a fighter and I win.*

Up ahead, just as they said, was movement. I squinted. It looked like an animal, maybe.

"Life," I said, somewhat impressed.

So, I ran closer, to get a better look. When I got it, I stopped dead in my tracks.

I was still twenty feet away but refused to get a foot closer. I could see the thing clearly now, with its scarred skin, mouthless, eyeless face. It moaned in an agony that its vestigial mouth couldn't fully realize. It was a man, I realized.

His skin was a mass of scar tissue, pulled tight around his skull, leaving the features of his species exposed, but unrealized. His lips, somehow, had grown together, and although he tried to speak, he could not. His jaws moved impotently behind the sheet of skin that was his face. Each of his limbs were truncated, by nature or will. I couldn't tell for sure. But he was crawling on what was left of his fours, mewling. The impression I had of the man, the creature, was absolute agony. Terrible, terrible agony.

Instinctively, I raised the gun.

"I think you have the right idea, mate," said Tomlin. "I don't think you'll hear that from me so often."

"What happened to it?" asked Wilhelmina.

I shrugged. I didn't know if anything happened to it. I didn't know if it was the only life form here, or if there were more of them just like that.

It looked up at me and let out a muffled mewling.

"Should I do it, then?"

"It's in pain. I'd rather meet oblivion than be... *that*."

Despite not having any eyes, I could've sworn the thing winced, reacting in some way. I aimed at its head and tried to still the pounding in my chest. I took a deep breath and held the air in my lungs. I pulled the trigger.

The gun kicked back in my hand and the thing whipped about violently for a moment, tossing and turning like a snake on a hot road. I shot its brain, but I had the sudden terrible idea that it might have more brains inside of it, that I was assuming too much of what it was. But it never came alive again, it just laid there, eventually, red blood oozing from its skull.

I wiped my brow and tucked the pistol into my belt line.

The others looked down at the ground, as if they were sharing a moment of silence for the scarred, limbless thing.

"Where to next?" I said. I was trying to make a joke, but no one said anything. No one laughed.

I knew where we were going next.

There was one tower, in the middle of the city, that was larger than the rest, seeming to touch the sky. It was burnt black and impossibly tall. Chunks torn from its side revealed iron rebar, overgrown with twisting vines. I pulled out my notes. My envelope was largely useless to me in the real world, but here I made sense of Dr. Gossam's scribblings. He had a page of notes for me, distinct from the rest. Where everything else he supplied me with was typed and lucid, this yellow page was written with the feverish intensity of a medium channeling the dead. On it were a series of words and phrases, none of which made sense up above.

But, so below...

Black city bombed. High tower. The Golden King sits.

I swallowed.

"We're close."

11.

S tanding in front of it, we were frozen. It'd have taken a seismic force to move us. The longer I stayed in the Black City, the more I wondered if I could ever leave. I looked at Tomlin and Wilhelmina with even more suspicion. What did I need them for?

"How do we get out of here?" I asked.

Wilhelmina shook her head. "Who knows if we do."

"Don't bloody say that."

"Karkarr said a gateway would open," said Tomlin. "Don't you trust him?"

"I don't know," I said. "But they need to get D'Ambrosere back somehow."

We stepped into the lobby of the great building. We'd seen shapes slithering about on our walk, more scarred up humanoids desperately crawling toward some unknown goal. I didn't bother putting them out of their misery. Regret had already begun to swirl in my thoughts. Something didn't sit right with me about my execution, like I'd fucked with something I didn't understand. For all I knew, its warbling, muffled cries of pain could've been a greeting.

Put that aside. You're being paranoid.

I focused. I breathed.

The building's lobby was sparse, minimalist. There were disemboweled couches and a concierge desk. I assumed there'd be employee restrooms too.

"This a hotel?" I said aloud.

"A parody," said Wilhelmina. "It's made up like a hotel, but serves no function. It's like an exaggerated copy. An impression."

"Fucking hell," said Tomlin.

"When I get back, I'm going to strangle the good doctor."

"As long as he pays us first."

"Do you think there's an elevator?"

As if on cue, we all saw the polished silver at the end of the room.

"Reckon it works?"

"I'm not sure we should even try," said Wilhelmina. But she didn't mean it. She was practically whispering: *go on, try it. Go go go go go.*

"We don't even know where to go," said Tomlin. *Up up up up.*

"If you were the Golden King, where would you place your throne?"

The doors opened.

"Going up?" I said.

I think we were all surprised that it actually worked, that when we pressed the button for the top floor it came to life, lit up and everything. It shook and hummed, and we felt the sensation of movement, however contained. It worked. None of us could believe it, but somehow, it unsettled us even more. Or maybe it was just me. The other two stood close together, their fingers intertwined.

This place, this Black City, was as close to Hell as we could imagine—just as Dr. Gossam said. I did not know if Allosaurus D'Ambrosere came here on his own accord or was taken, but the concept of not only being here, but being a king here, frightened me.

The Golden King.

The others didn't talk, but I hoped we were thinking the same things.

Nausea swept over me when the door opened. I didn't want to see.

Red light pierced my eyes and cold wind rushed toward me, cutting through to my bones. How could a place so red be so cold?

We stepped out into the light and realized now that thunder was roaring, crashing, screaming. The windows had all been shattered and when the red sky flashed with white light, it felt as if we could reach out and touch the energy with our own hands.

It was raining. In the blackness of the floor, which opened up into a broken cliff a thousand feet above the Black City, we could smell it.

And we all saw it too. The silhouette that stood against the endless bloody cosmos. A man.

"Are you—" I felt stupid saying it. "Are you Allosaurus D'Ambrosere?"

There was a short pause, then the man said, "My name, in my time, was merely unusual. Now, I'm afraid, it's absurd. Please, call me Al."

12.

A cid rain fell with the grace of dump trucks. Balls of lightning illuminated black clouds. Thunder growled in the distance. Tomlin came up beside me, and I thought, maybe, for a moment, he was there to protect me. Wilhelmina came to my other side and I felt as if we were all a trio for once. That everything had come together, and just as well.

"How do we get you back, Al?" I said.

And that's when they grabbed me on both sides.

"I think you'll figure it out," he said. I never saw his face.

Tomlin was big, strong. He couldn't fight worth a damn, but when he held me, I couldn't move. Wilhelmina on the other hand, every time she put her hands on me, I shook them off. I was like an eel, slippery. But she didn't need me to stay put, she just needed me still enough to pull my gun from my waistband.

"You should've backed out," she whispered. "We wanted you to back out."

"Left us no choice, mate. No hard feelings," muttered Tomlin.

The man named Al was still shrouded in shadows, looking out upon the Black City. He didn't turn around to hear my cries, my sharp yelps, my violently flailing elbows.

Tomlin held me in a bear hug while Wilhelmina made distance. Soon, it didn't matter who was holding me—the gun's barrel did plenty of work on its own.

I swallowed. I watched my partners from the corner of my eye. They looked as whipped and gutless as they had before, only now there was no turning back.

I stopped struggling. Wilhelmina had her finger on the trigger.

"So, what is this?" I said.

D'Ambrosere turned from the window and seemed to glide toward me. He was wearing long golden robes that hid the mediocre fitness of a jolly fifty-year old man. It was the first time I got a look at him. He seemed a pleasant fellow in different circumstances. His beard was gray, his spectacles stylish, he had a large frame and a wicked smile. He reminded me a little of Orson Welles, but not the young man—the fat guy who showed up on game shows. I looked him in his crystal blue eyes and suddenly felt sick to my stomach.

"I'm afraid I don't know your name."

"I came here to rescue you."

"That's not your name."

"Byron."

He said it aloud, tasting it on his lips. "Well, Byron, it's good to meet you. And your friends?"

They said their names and D'Ambrosere nodded dutifully. "Very good," he said. "And which of my esteemed colleagues sent you?"

Wilhelmina answered, to my surprise. "Dr. Gossam."

I could feel Tomlin's hot breath on the back of my neck. I realized, quickly, that I was an idiot.

"He came to you two first," I said.

"We really hoped we wouldn't make it this far," he said, his voice shaking.

I replayed it all in my head. All the way back to Clarence's smug smile. *That fucking prick.*

Wilhelmina pulled out a scrap of paper. "Gossam said you'd know what this means."

Al took the paper in his hands, squinted and then nodded. "Why, yes. I believe I do. It's almost time." He looked at me, his Gateway, and sighed. "I really will miss it here."

And then I remembered everything else. Karkarr's gateway. The strained form, the elastic flesh, the vaginal slit running from sternum to crotch. I tried to block out the thought, the pain. I tried to block out everything about that experience, the one that I'd soon be feeling. Al brought a knife from his robes. He came toward me smoothly, like a serpent. He looked at me as if I wasn't a man, but some beast. A pig meant for the slaughter.

"I really must thank you," he said. "It's no small feat leaving, but really it is quite a pain to come back. But now that we've figured it out, this will be no small revolution. This world, the one you stand in now, will be able to colonize ours, just as it colonized me."

For just a moment, I thought I saw the red from the sky reflected in his eyes.

Twisting, biting, cursing—I made Allosaurus leap back. Tomlin still had me and I couldn't do shit but struggle. Until I dropped low, that is. Until, I slipped through his arms, to the floor on bent knees, then rocketed myself up into his jaw, my skull cracking as it made contact. Tomlin released me and just as he did—

BLAM!

Orange light.

Sharp pain.

Wilhelmina squeezed off shot two behind a cloud of gun smoke. I was already scrambling on the ground. I held my arm and felt a hot stickiness seeping through my clothes.

D'Ambrosere watched this all with distant amusement.

When the second shot rang out, it hit right beside me, throwing up a mist of plaster, wood, and chalk from the floor. The elevator opened, I thought about it, but another gunshot had me veering right as sparks exploded in front of me. As I ran for the stairwell, I wondered how this place existed, for the hundredth time, and distantly D'Ambrosere yelled, "Get him!"

The stairs were too steep, too narrow. They weren't like regular stairs. They looked like stairs you'd see in a nightmare version of architecture. Behind me, footsteps. Three of them. Or maybe just two. I wasn't sure if Al walked anymore. For all I knew that motherfucker was a constant inch off the earth. I held on to the rickety railing and tried to ignore the blood and the pain in my arm as I leapt from flight to flight, tucking and rolling to lessen the impact. Soon, there were thirty floors below me and another twenty above. I was almost halfway there and my whole body hurt, a dull muscle pain that encompassed my whole existence nicely. It smothered the sharp pain of the bullet wound. But, I couldn't give too much of a shit about that right now, because the footsteps above me were growing louder and I knew they wouldn't let me go for anything.

I was their way out, after all.

A bullet whistled past my ear as I ran to the main floor. I was sure that they were only two flights behind me. By the time I got to the street, into the rain, my side hurt too. I was wheezing. I wasn't sure how much further I could go.

But, have you ever seen what happens when it rains?

My mind flashed back to the days of my childhood. Back in Seattle when I was a British kid in the States and not the other way around. It'd rain there all the time. It'd rain so much you don't even think about it. Kind of like England, in a way. But I remembered going out to the garden, after it rained, under the cover of a rainbow, to see a dozen slugs oozing out from wherever they hid to rest on our patio. I was both disgusted and enamored by these things.

Looking back, I'm not sure if it was the rain that pulled the city's citizens out of their hidden homes, but they were out on the streets all the same.

Ahead of me: a deformed humanoid, totally nude, with a jaw full of crystalline teeth.

I spun.

Behind me: a pack of shambling beings on all fours, their legs long and unnaturally limber. I realized they were everywhere—and now one of them was dead.

Did they understand murder?

Did they know that I was their murderer?

The thought flushed my spine with ice water.

Each of these beings were missing something. Eyes, noses, lips, limbs. They were all hairless and their tissue was thick with damage. They were the product of science fiction—a warning of nuclear apocalypse. Something to scare the tykes into giving peace a chance.

Maybe.

Whatever they were, they started toward me. And behind me, I heard Tomlin yell, all bluster and bloodlust, "There 'e is!"

Wilhelmina lined up another shot, but Al was right behind her. "No! Don't shoot! We need him!" Then, he looked down at his scrap of paper and made some silent mutterings. "We've only got ten minutes," he said. "Roughly."

If I hadn't been so scared, if I hadn't been running like a madman, I'd have considered that more thoroughly. I would've sat and listened to my body and tried to contemplate what I felt growing inside me. Did we all have one of these, at one point or another? Has a child been eviscerated by a glass pane, only to reveal a flashing violet light? Has a bereaved mother ever climbed inside her child to live the rest of her days in the Black City?

I ran, fast, faster than I'd ever ran. I was losing blood and I was sore all over, but I still ran. There was nothing left to do. I dodged past the locals who seemed to vocalize from their stomachs, low growls that mixed with thunder. They lunged at me as I passed. Each time I turned down a new street, I heard their raw flesh slapping on the ground in pursuit.

Quickly, I stumbled into an open storefront, running past empty shelves. *Why was this place like this? Why did they need shelves? What did these people eat? Who was Allosaurus D'Ambrosere to them?*

I already had the answer though: *The Golden King.*

Who knew what he'd been doing here all these years. Who knew what this place was to him, or these people.

The store slowed them down—they all had to funnel through a door—so as soon as I was out the other side, I dipped into another across the street. Pride beamed inside of me. *I was doing it, I was going to get away.* At least for now.

I turned into an alley, something that looked like a blackened set from one of those New York movies, all gray skies and rats as big as steaks. There was a dumpster, filled with trash—although I wasn't sure where it was from. Beside the dumpster was a flight of wire stairs and I climbed them as fast as I could, hurting so bad that I thought I might vomit.

The rain peppered my face. I ran up the stairs. Was this my whole life now? Running up and down stairs? Scrambling for mercy in the Black City?

I knew that if I were a portal, a gateway, that I wouldn't be forever. They'd have to leave me alone at a certain point. I didn't know the specifics, but I knew that it was as much luck as it was chance. There was only a small window where they could slit me open and crawl inside and go home.

A hand smashed through a window. Scarred and pink, its fingernails chewed off. The thing it was attached to crawled after me.

I screamed and kicked. When it lunged again I grabbed its skull and beat it into the brick wall beside us, letting it froth at its embryonic mouth, as its dome caved in and red, red blood gushed from its blank white eyes.

None of them looked quite like the others, I realized.

I wondered now if this was by design or by chance.

Did chance even exist anymore?

The rain washed the blood from my hands, a pink memory, as I reached the rooftop.

I collapsed.

There was no more running left in me. There was no more fight.

I heard the scrambling of the locals. I heard the yelling of my London comrades. Up above, I stared into the sky to try to see if it was the same one I used to stare at.

Crawling on my hands and knees, I looked out over the city from my modest perch. Everyone was working together. They were coming toward me. Al, Tomlin, and Wilhelmina were pointing and shouting. They saw me. I blinked.

There they were, and there I was: in the court of the Golden King.

Did I ever tell you about why I had to leave the States?

13.

I was eighteen and I had a bit of a greaser thing going, real James Dean. I thought I was hot shit, especially when I could still drudge up my old accent and say things that sounded English. Girls liked that back then, guys did too. Some of them anyways.

Seattle wasn't a big cool town back then, and I didn't know why my parents decided to take me.

"Just in time," said Allosaurus D'Ambrosere. He held a knife with a twisting blade above his head.

"Are we all going?"

"Yes, indeed."

But Dad got a job here and that's all there was to it. Sometimes, Dads get jobs and you're just stuck, you know? So, I did my fair share of cruising. I was part of a rough group, and we had a bit of a gang, but really it was just kid shit. We stole beer and cigarettes and smashed bottles, and sometimes we'd jump someone if we were feeling really up to it, but mostly our stuff was small-scale juvenile delinquent shit.

By the time I was eighteen, my parents had enough of me. They were determined to end my reign of terror, so they told me they'd send me to this school, this military school. I told them I was done with this shitty town, that I wanted to go back home. It didn't matter that I'd lived in Seattle a lot longer than England, the States just solidified my identity.

Wilhelmina kicked me in the stomach. I wasn't going to fight back. Too tired.

Tomlin's big black disc of an eye stared down at me from above. "I can't wait to see him squirm."

"You won't wait long."

But, there was this guy. I'd just discovered my omnivorous nature recently, fooling around with a fellow gang member named Jerry. Jerry was cute, a tough looking Jewish kid with curly black hair. He was the first boy to kiss me. We'd go off alone sometimes, and I'd tell him about my life and he'd ruffle my hair and we'd trade blowjobs and it was really just good fun. Two guys, fooling around. But then things got a little heavy one night.

I was thinking about staying then, because things were getting normal. Things were feeling good. I'd just gotten a job and my parents were calming down about the whole school thing.

I looked up bewildered, the Golden King held court around me. A hundred uniquely disfigured humanoids joined us on the rooftop.

"What are you going to do when you get back?"

"Sell some books."

Well, one night we went out of town a little, to this hiking trail. It was beautiful, a great spot to get into some shit, if you know what I mean. For some reason, I think we both knew this was going to be the night we'd try full on sex. It didn't take much for us to think that—we were guys, after all. We liked to fuck.

We got on the trail and our hands were all over each other, pulling each other apart. I don't think I ever loved anyone more than Jerry at that moment.

Afterwards, on that warm summer night, we lay in each other's arms, staring up at the sky.

I could make out the faint outlines of stars. My shoulder hurt. I was still bleeding.

"We'll have to do this quickly. He's wasted too much time."

And we saw a flashlight. A single circle of white light bobbing in the forest.

Of course, we were scared. But Jerry kissed me on the cheek and I saw something else in him. Pride.

He looked at me and I knew he was going to stand up, make something of it. But the light flashed toward us before we could do anything.

"Well, well, well, look at what we have here."

There was no denying it. We were both men, both nude. Both dripping with each other's spoor. The man was hunting, probably illegally. He had a rifle slung on his back. This was just a hiking trail, a national forest. At night. He shouldn't have been here.

He had the rifle in his hands, but Jerry, the maniac, already had a rock in his own and before the rifle was at chest level, the rock smacked the man in the eye. Jerry had a good throw like that, he was a baseball pitcher in school. He had a mean fastball.

I didn't know what I was doing, but I was following his lead. I stood up and ran for the guy, who was now throwing the bolt to his rifle. Jerry was already on him, and I knew one of us was going to die tonight.

For that moment, I didn't care.

"Where are we going to go?"

D'Ambrosere shrugged, "Wherever he'll take us. Back."

I wanted to kill that bastard too, not just because he caught us, but because Jerry wanted to. I wanted to be more like Jerry than I wanted to be like anyone in my whole life. More than James Dean or Michael Landon, I wanted to be Jerry. So, it was easy to throw a couple punches at the guy's face, easy to spatter his brains out on the forest floor.

For a moment, we were all three wrestling, and we were all still alive, all fighting viciously for survival and I knew that's the only way there was to fight. I wanted to be trapped in that moment forever, that struggle.

A thunderous crack broke us apart. Our interloper found the trigger and pulled.

Jerry rolled off of him. There were no long goodbyes. No stories. No myths. Nothing to write about Jerry. Just a queer killed in the woods. He died instantly. I think the bullet caught him in the heart.

I kicked the gun away and put my full weight on the guy's head, crushing it, tears rolling down my cheeks. He kept hitting at me, but his hits kept getting weaker too. He couldn't do shit, not when I was like this. I lifted my body up off the ground and slammed my weight into him again and again. If anyone would've seen us, a naked boy killing a man...I probably would've been shot on sight.

Eventually, the man stopped moving.

Jerry was naked and beautiful and totally lifeless.

And I was just a kid, you know? I didn't know what to do.

Tomlin and Wilhelmina stood on my wrists as the knife pierced my skin. I felt it travel down, parting me like the red sea. I screamed, but they weren't listening. They didn't give a shit. I could feel whatever it was roiling inside me. I was blooming. My flesh was already beginning to shift and vibrate.

I ran along the trail and the night sky was above me, that beautiful night sky, and I was covered in blood and semen. I was going to leave, I decided. I had to run. I was a kid, after all. There was nothing else to do but run.

For the first time, though, with Jerry, I felt I was home. This was my home. And I was leaving.

My guts rearranged, forced apart by something I didn't understand. Dozens of faces glowered over me, ready to climb inside, to return to whence they came.

Take me there.

THE MOURNER ACROSS THE FLAMES

Scott J. Moses

The Emissary

T he shot rang out across the salt, and Bharath peered through the rifle's scope at the two travelers stopped cold. As the rifle's roar faded, undulating echoes to the mountains where salt met cerulean sky, the two mule-mounted travelers, rags swaddling their faces, looked to one another, their mules unfazed by the interruption. The shot was a warning, but Bharath jerked back the bolt-action, ejecting the shell, and forced in another. Salt flowed in phantasmal wisps, floating atop the countryside like gusts of powdered snow. Though Bharath only knew snow's likeness from stories, from those ancient enough to recall it. He leaned into the salt bags, brought his eye to the scope again.

The leader's head swiveled to his companion, their goggles glinting sunstare once, twice, then back to the tower where Bharath crouched, death in his hands.

Four mules for two zealots? Bharath thought, and slowed his breathing, homed his sights on the one dismounting. The leader advanced a step, then another, their hands raised to the amorphous clouds, and as they crept to the corpse a mule's length away, aflood with feasting buzzards big as a child, Bharath grit his teeth beneath his cloth mask.

"Could you take him from here?" said a soft voice behind him.

"Yes, Love."

"Like the dead one there? All the others?"

"Yes."

The figure neared the corpse, their shawl whipping in the harsh wind, and Bharath let loose another round. The buzzards screamed, scrambling off on shambled wings as the dead man skidded along the salt flats, sliding to a halt. The zealot nearest the corpse had flown back, as if they were the one shot, and sat there now, chest heaving as the salt blew in plumes.

The zealot stood, brushing the salt from themselves in futility, and motioned to the one still mounted behind him. They turned their back to the tower, and Bharath clocked the rifle slung over their shoulder. The zealot turned from their companion and cupped hands around their mouth, though Bharath couldn't quite make the words. Their call all but smothered on the roaring wind.

"Will more come?" The voice behind him again. *"More like the dead the salt preserves for the demon birds?"*

"I suspect so," Bharath said, willing the zealot to pull his rifle like all the others. "Though I'm surprised they still come in pairs."

Bharath thought he heard his name where the salt met the sky. He looked to the horizon, squinting in the sun's onslaught despite his goggles, heard his name once more. He ejected the spent shell, fed his rifle another, and when he brought his eye to the scope again, the figure had removed their cloth-mask, goggles flung to the white-laden earth. Bharath smirked, dialing the man's head between his crosshairs.

"Don't," the voice whispered. *"Please..."*

Bharath's teeth sawed behind his lips watching Kamber turn back to his companion, perhaps wondering if they might die like those sent before. Never to rot, but to be preserved in the purified desert. One enormous feast for the morning carrion-eaters.

Kamber took the rifle from his back. Bharath tensed, finger caressing the trigger, and pulled the stock tight to his shoulder, stopped when Kamber dropped the rifle to the salt at his feet. The wind rose again, a steady wail through the tower's open-faced view. They all looked to Bharath now, the mules, their masters.

"They *would* send him," Bharath said. "Cowards."

A hand gripped his shoulder, squeezed. *"Hear his words, for me?"*

Bharath sighed and lowered his rifle. Standing, he made his way to a large circular mirror in the window near him. He tilted it so that it gathered sun, did this three times before leaving it brimmed with light. He crouched behind the bags again, took up his rifle, watched.

The travelers brought their hands to their faces, and Kamber bent low, though for his goggles or rifle, Bharath didn't know. It mattered little, Bharath was prepared to kill him, *longed* for circumstance to force his hand. Kamber stopped short, seeming to wisen, and mounted his mule. He turned back to his companion, motioning before they advanced. Bharath watched them until they passed the corpse, and as the screaming buzzards returned to their meal, he leaned his rifle to the wall, placed his hand over the smaller one still gripping his shoulder, felt the nothing there.

Bharath slipped on his leather cuirass. The room bare of anyone, save himself.

The Proposition

B	harath kept his rifle close as he wound the pulley, feeding the salt-riddled rope through the mechanism lowering the platform he stood upon. *Of course they'd send him*, he thought, watching them and their mules stopped in the shade of the tower's shadow.

When he was mere feet above the salt, he released the pulley, and the metal platform slammed to the earth with a violent *clang*, sending vibrations up through his boots and legs. Bharath breathed heavily through his facial covering, eyeing Kamber and the one atop the mule through his goggles. As Kamber stepped forward, Bharath lifted his rifle.

The salt blew in ethereal wisps, and along the horizon, the demon buzzards had returned to the flung corpse. The last emissary of three sent from the settlement Bharath had put down. The mule bearing the rider shook its head, snorted.

Kamber's risen arms trembled, his flowing robes whipping in the wind's onslaught. "How many will you kill, Bharath? How many to ensure retribution? You test their patience."

Bharath allowed Kamber to lower his arms, enjoyed how slowly he did so. "All they must do is come to the edge of the salt where the corpses lay strewn. All five of them. Then, and *only then*, will I be done."

"You're insane," Kamber said, chuckling, shoulders shaking with his words. He extended his hand, stepped forward. Bharath raised his rifle again.

"Stop there, dead man," Bharath said, gaze flicking from the hunched one atop the mule to Kamber. *Not one of them*, he thought. *Someone else.*

"All of us are dead, Bharath. Matter of time, is all."

"Then speak, dead man."

Kamber glanced over his shoulder to his companion, still in mask and goggles. They looked frail. "I come on behalf of the Pillar. A final proposition. If—"

"On behalf of the Pillar…" Bharath shook his head. "Can you hear yourself? Traitor. Unfriend. *We* allowed her to die…but *you*, her blood…you most of all."

Kamber stilled. "And what would *Sarai* say? Hmm? Look at you, living on the outskirts among the carrion, the scavengers, the salt. What would my sister say, Bharath? *Tell me.*"

Bharath gripped the rifle tight. "She says plenty. She's the reason you're not a corpse like all the others. She stayed my hand, she—"

"Sarai doesn't *say anything* anymore," Kamber said, voice a growl. He looked to the salt at his feet. "She's gone, Bharath… Don't you see? You're sick from your time with the stone in that cell. You're hearing voices, those who

86

aren't there." He stepped forward, and Bharath allowed him the gained ground. "The Pillar, they cured me with the Brine. They'll cure you *too*, if only you stop this madness."

"I stop when they're dead," Bharath said, the rifle's stock firm against his shoulder.

Kamber sighed, and turned to the one behind him who remained still. "Fool, this one. I wish you luck, I do." Kamber looked back to Bharath. "Here's what the Pillar offers, a last chance for recompense. I pray you listen, lest me or the high one Herself is ordered to return with twenty zealots to end you entirely. Prove you're not some heretic on the cusp of madness, if not for you, *her*. Do this for Sarai, if you ever loved her at all."

Bharath spoke down the sights of his rifle. "I'm the only one who did."

Kamber balled his fists, and Bharath prayed he would.

Kamber straightened. "You are to lead this one here to the base of the mountains at the salt's edge. He is to be protected, led there to bury his family. Your Fetcher has permission to grant you additional supplies for the journey. Do this, and you will be given audience with the Pillar, born to the Brine once more. Given leave to live out your days as a Fetcher, or perhaps, a zealot, in peace."

"Peace…" Bharath said, and opened his mouth to continue. Kamber spoke first.

"The Fetcher is instructed to refuse supplies if this one is not with you upon arrival. You have four days, beginning morrow morning, to lead him there and safely back. Questions?"

Bharath looked past Kamber to the rider, who took down his cloth mask, lifted his goggles. An old man, lines like trenches creased throughout his gaunt face. He shook as the salt peppered his robes. Behind him, bound by hefts of rope and bent over the mule, were two figures wrapped in cloth. Bharath knew the smell well, and for a moment saw Sarai in the shaman's quarters. The black of plague spilling from her eyes, nose, her—

"Four days," Kamber said, as many fingers held high. "Then I, or She, return with armed zealots. We have been instructed to kill you, the mourner, and your Fetcher if the task is incomplete."

Bharath held his breath, couldn't take his eyes from the dead across the mule. He lowered his rifle. "And I will be rid of this place? Granted audience with them?"

Kamber leaned into his words. Bharath thought he saw tears. "And *cured*. See reason, friend, for my sister, the love you had for her."

Bharath white-knuckled his rifle as the traitor turned back to his mount.

Before pulling himself onto his mule, he tied the second's reins to a dried, wooden stake impaled in the ground. He held his fingers skyward again, then turned, trotting off, leaving Bharath with the old man whose eyes never left his own.

Bharath's rifle rose, its mouth trained on Kamber's bobbing form. He drew in air, puffed his cheeks, blew. *"Poooow,"* he said, mimicking the rifle's kick, and lowering the weapon, he glimpsed the old man again, still staring.

"Make camp near the tower's base," Bharath said, stepping onto the metal platform, hands gripping the pulley. "Cast a fire, so the demons don't think you dead."

The mourner's sunken eyes were small and dark. The mules seemed to stare as well, seemed to share those gray, lifeless eyes. The old man lifted his head and salt fell from his wild hair.

"I don't know you from *them*," Bharath said. "So you won't sleep above. We'll set off with sunrise." He cranked the pulley once, twice, and the platform rose with a metallic whine. He stopped then, sight stuck to the corpses on the mule again. "How did they die?" Bharath asked, knowing the answer.

The old man craned his neck to those strapped behind him, and swiveled back to Bharath. He ran his bone-fingers down his eyes, nose, and mouth.

Bharath saw her then, drenched in sweat. Dark hair soaked through and moaning in that floor-level cot. Black in lines from her eyes, the skin of her amber forehead peeling like dried vegetables.

Bharath's throat tightened, and he gripped the wheel. The gears groaned as the platform resumed its ascent. He leaned over the edge. "Don't forget that fire."

The old man's gaze the only reply.

Bharath lay awake, his eyes on the rusted-metal ceiling. The moonlight seeped through its many wounds, bathing the room a deep blue.

He believed I conceded, Bharath thought, and turned to the sun-bleached skeleton propped against the wall near the salt bags where his rifle rested.

This was the closest he'd come these months to getting the Pillar in his sights. He had more than enough ammunition, but the journey was long, requiring more supplies than the usual allotment. Bharath sighed and met the skeleton's eyeless sockets. He could just make out where the skull had been ravaged by the bullet, still see the darkness on the wall where the blood, brain, and bone burst outward.

"It's easy," the skeleton whispered, mouth in a silent scream. *"So easy. The flatlands, this tower…theirs, understand? You rebel as I did, but never forget it was they who placed you here."*

Bharath rolled over, facing the wall, and in the quiet, he heard her.

"I'm lonely."

He could almost see her there, between him and the stacked-stone wall. Her slender outline lit blue by the moonlight. Her bronze skin gleaming.

Bharath reached for her, breath caught in his lungs, and recoiled, his breathing rapid. "This isn't real," he said. "You're not here."

Sarai sighed, and ran a hand through her hair, turning away from him. Despite himself, he reached for her again, as he always did. The skeleton whispered behind him.

"It's nice. You'll see…"

Sarai now. *"What is reality if not what one perceives?"*

Bharath growled, covering his eyes as the tears came. Perhaps Kamber was right? Perhaps the sickness was coming to fruition? What power had the stone to make him hear and see the unreal? Could he really crawl back now, to the Pillar? They who might make the voices stop?

No, he thought. *They must pay.*

He would be off to see the Fetcher come morning, would try to convince him, as he had these last weeks, that they were prisoners. Both of them—

A scratching at the outer wall.

Bharath sat up, the moon dimmer now, and though he could see the bone-thin hand, its much too long fingers, clasping the inner edge of the window, he willed it away until a liquid snarl rose amidst the outer darkness. Bharath recoiled back at the emaciated thing standing there, each thin appendage grasping the stone and salt bags for purchase. A gaunt figure, the height of a man, its eyes gleaming like muzzle-flare. Mouth ajar, opening wide, wider, wider still—jutting teeth like upturned beaks glinting in the moonlight.

Bharath jerked at Sarai's touch. *"What is it, love?"* She rubbed his arm, her hand warm.

"Stay behind me. There's—"

And when he peered through the tower's opening again, only the ink-blue sky met his gaze. The night filled with ember stars.

No one, nothing.

Sweat poured from him, and he threw the sheet aside, stood there naked as the skeleton cackled to itself. All as it ever was. Bharath's breathing slowed, and he turned to the skeleton propped where it'd been since they'd led him here. A question on his lips. *Did you see?* But the former tenant was still, silent, and as the wind blew in from the salt flats, Bharath caught the orange glimmer reflected on the metal roofing above where his rifle lay.

Kamber in his mind then: *"You're sick, Bharath. First voices, now, this?"*

His legs grew weak, and Bharath touched his fingers to his eyes, drew them back, and saw the plague there.

Sarai in that cot, black in lines from her eyes, nose, and lips. Her hands clawing at her throat and legs, attempting to free herself of her skin.

The old man making those lines down his eyes.

How Sarai had visions at the end, heard voices. Screamed in that decrepit room he was barred from.

I can't die, not yet, Bharath thought, and looked to the rust-pocked ceiling again, to the more-than-like nothing god dwelling above the metal there. *Why grant me resiliency in the cell, with the stone, if only to kill me now, when I'm close? Let me live to—*

"Live to what, love?" Sarai wrapped her arms around him from behind, and he leaned into her kiss.

"Nothing, love," he said, "you needn't worry." And glimpsing the orange-red dancing along the roof again, he made his way to the salt bags, hand in Sarai's all the while. Peeking out over the fortifications, Bharath watched the old man in the light of his small fire. He stood by the dead strapped to the mule—his family—head bent to them, perhaps kissing them where the cloth had been pulled away to reveal fishbelly skin. Bharath thought to take up his rifle, to bring it to his eye to better decipher the old man's lips, make out what he said in the dark. The flame cast shadows around him, breaking to either side of the frail one as he cooed. The mules awake as well, heads turned and surveying all as Bharath did.

"It would be unkind," Sarai said. *"Let him mourn, love. Think if it were me strapped to that mule."*

"Of course," Bharath said, watching the old man caress the lifeless. How he buried his face against their bare skin, trembling. The semi-audible whispers climbing the tower's walls. The flames undulated, lashing out in their way. The surrounding shadows in continuous transfiguration.

Bharath smiled, despite it all, and felt the warmth of Sarai's breath on his neck. Perhaps he would see the mourner bury his family. It would be easier—if Kamber could be believed—if he were welcomed back. Even as a servant, he would be close to them. Bharath grimaced and drew his hand back from the black sludge coating the wall's edge. A slithering pool in the crevices of the stonework. He brought the hand to his face, clean as it ever was.

The Fetcher

T he sun shimmered on the salt like glass as the platform touched the earth. Bharath stepped off, watching the old man draw back from the mule and the two figures it bore.

He speaks to them, Bharath thought. *Like they're still alive.* He tore the last heft of Brine meat in two, held it to the old man.

"Here," Bharath said. "The Fetcher is close, but not so much as to not have something in you."

The old man stared, his lips cracked and dry. The lines near the corners of his eyes trenches. The goggles atop his head engulfed his shrunken skull.

Is he ill? Bharath thought, moving to the supply mule, which held the last of his collected rain water in a skin tied to its back and the grain brought from the settlement.

Only enough for the task at hand. Even in rebellion, I am theirs. Bharath grit his teeth, and the smoke of the mourner's doused fire rose in lines to the blue sky above.

After prepping the mules, Bharath mounted the one with the fewest items: two bedrolls, and two empty sacks for what the Fetcher was to give them. He watched the old man, whispering again to the corpses behind him.

Perhaps, he tells them they'll be safe, Bharath thought.

"Eavesdropper."

Bharath jerked around to no one. Though he'd heard her. Knew he had.

He shook his head, and looked to the old man who, one arthritic hand on his mule's reins, tossed the flap back over the larger of the two dead. The mourner wiped his mouth, and the pair sat there a moment, eyeing one another.

Bharath clicked his tongue. With a snort, the mules set off.

Bharath smelled it first, that sour, sulfur stench of the dead lake shimmering green, stretching to the mountains beyond. He glanced back at the old man and nodded to the black, wide bubbling pits which had grown in number since leaving the tower. He pointed to the goop and shook his head at the old man, while directing his mule around each in turn.

An amalgamation of wood and metal slabs stood before them, the likes of which were fashioned into an open-facing, three-walled workshop. A mouth wide to the lake. A long-doused fire pit, lush with ash and burnt driftwood lay at the camp's center, and in the half-dome structure's side, lay the Fetcher's living quarters. Spartan: a bed—void of blankets or pillow—a desk, and mat. The rest of the workshop filled with the exoskeletons of what the Fetcher did with his days. Hulking shells, an inch thick, durable, yet light, stood as if they may still be alive. Their huge eyes, the size of a man's fist, their bodies easily the size of a mule in height and length. Cloth tarps hung lazily before the workshop's entrance, and as Bharath dismounted his mule, the old man did as well.

Staring the length of the shore, Bharath saw the Fetcher in his rusted armor, sitting atop a large mound of stone, the crank-pulley of the Brine trap at his side and made of crude driftwood. A chain extended from the mechanism, taut and swallowed beneath that dead water, where a large red sphere bobbed atop the slow-moving stillness.

Bharath turned to the old man. "Best let him finish."

The cloth draped before the entrance whipped violently in the gale as it roared through the camp, made loud by the cupped architecture of the Fetcher's workshop. The gust rattled metal, kicked up salt and sand along the shoreline, peppering the pair and their mules. Pockets of the bubbling ooze, black as sin, littered the shore in growing density. The stench more potent than their journey in.

Bharath scrunched his nose, and saw himself in their cell again. *The stone in the prison's center bright and glowing, that same metallic stench clawing in at his sanity, which all but buckled as he lay there, thinking of Sarai. Of how he longed for death.*

The red sphere sunk beneath the water and launched upward, again and again, while the heavy chain strained, unmoving. The Fetcher was on his feet, gloved hands to the sky in silent prayer. Bharath sighed. *I have to try. He may see yet…*

The Fetcher cranked the pulley nearest the chain, and it groaned, receding into the contraption beside him. Chain lurched from the water, more, more now, the *chinkchink-chink* piercing as hammered stakes, until Bharath saw the clasped jaws of the cage. The water was a maelstrom of violence as the insectoid legs of the Brine clawed out from the bars and teeth of the Fetcher's trap. Its legs shot out of the water, claws clenching and unclenching. It stopped—started again—kicking up the once-dormant waters dusted with salt.

The Fetcher locked the mechanism in place, took up the crude, two-handed sword, and made for the storm. Despite the thing's protest, he walked into the water, up to his ankles, calves, knees, thighs—all the while the Brine's many pincers clawed at him and all else, thrashing for freedom. Bharath slid the rifle from his back, peering in the scope.

The Brine's claw glanced off the Fetcher's shoulder plate, and he pivoted, bringing the hulking blade down hard. The Brine's appendages straightened with each slash, and the Fetcher repeated the motion until its legs floated still on the now calm waters. The Fetcher stuck his sword into the earth behind him, the blade almost matching his height, and took up a nearby cart, making his way to the kill.

Is this my fate? Bharath thought. *To be as he? In and out of the water 'till the end of my days?* Bharath chuckled beneath his rag-mask. *No, he will hear me this time.*

The sound of feet padding along the salt drew Bharath's gaze behind him, to the old man slinking to one of the bubbling pools near an enclave of overhung rock.

"Hey," Bharath said, and the old man lurched upward, meeting his eyes. "That's irradiated. Toxic." He thought of the cell again, lying there, clawing the stone floor, his own blood-specked vomit, but cast the memory away. "It'll eat through you in seconds, hear? Stay away from it."

If the old man heard him, he didn't show it. Sighing, Bharath turned back to the shore, to the Fetcher who'd crossed half the distance between them. He ran hunched, his head low, a booming thud with every footfall, that gargantuan sword in his hands, dragging the blade's tip along the salt shore.

Bharath sheathed the rifle to his back, removed his facial covering and goggles. He waved his hands in the air, heart pounding with panic, exertion. The Fetcher slowed, hefted the sword to his shoulder in one fluid arc, blade jutting toward the lake, and walked the remaining distance. Bharath turned back to the old man still craning his neck to the bubbling filth, though further away than before. Bharath shook his head. *Hopeless.*

The Fetcher breached his camp, and Bharath raised a hand in greeting. The Fetcher stuck his weapon in the ground by the workshop's entrance and tore back a section of cloth curtain. Inside lay three Brine exoskeletons, their severed legs piled neatly like wood. Atop a long, stone slab by a monstrous furnace lay charred Brine meat in bulk. A quantity Bharath had never seen before.

"I'm told you're informed of our journey," Bharath said, but his eyes leapt back to the mounds of flesh on the slab. More than enough to get them to the settlement. If the three of them made for the Pillar…well, they might have a chance. To hell with Kamber, to hell with the Pillar's offer.

The Fetcher took two mounds of the white meat, placed them on cloth, and doused them in salt before enclosing the cuts within, tying off the top into a makeshift bundle.

The Fetcher ducked out from under the tarp over the shop's entrance, Brine meat in hand, and Bharath scoffed.

"It's four days," he said, pointing to the bundle. "That's what you normally give me while holed up alone in my tower. It's not enough, not for two of us."

The Fetcher paused, grew still.

Bharath threw up his hands. "Are they so convinced I'll leave? Where could I go?"

The thin slits in the Fetcher's rusted helm betrayed nothing. He was an armored void, an instrument fulfilling a function, but Bharath had to try.

"I know they take your tongues as part of the ritual, as penance to become what you are." Bharath stepped forward, and the Fetcher dropped the meat at his feet.

Bharath thrust a finger forward. "If I don't complete the journey, you, me"—Bharath gestured over his shoulder—"him, we're done. Dead, and for what? It's in your best interest to supply us, because if we fail, they'll come for you. Or do you even care? Are you so bound to their customs you'd forfeit your life?"

The Fetcher slowly straightened, his armored plates shifting in clinks. He lifted three fingers to the air, said nothing.

Bharath growled beneath his cloth-mask. "You see, Fetcher? This, all of it—your embankment camp, the tower they left me in—benefits *them*. We're jailed, don't you see?"

The Fetcher lowered one of his three fingers.

"How's life with no tongue? How many of your own blood suffer at their hand?" Bharath didn't care now. All that slow coercion, that calculated manipulation over the last weeks all but gone. "See how they cut pieces from us? They aim to make us less than who we are."

The Fetcher lowered another finger, yanked his sword up with his free-hand. Bharath stepped back, lifted his hands. "I know you know who I am: heretic… blasphemer… They probably said I'd try to turn you…and they're right. Though it's not even worth bringing up now, is it? You're truly theirs, aren't you?" Bharath eyed the meat again, more than enough to get them to the settlement, to give them the strength for what needed to be done. He turned, and pulled Kamber's rifle from the mule, threw it at the Fetcher's feet. Said the words:

"I give thanks to the Brine, who satisfy my needs in kind."

Bharath nodded to the flung rifle. "There's no scripture for Brine wine, so take the rifle. I'll have a skin of your best."

The Fetcher lowered his sword, the hulk's shoulders dropping as if he'd anticipated killing Bharath, and disappeared into the shop again.

Seems bootlegging is the extent of his rebellion. Pity…

The Fetcher reemerged from under the tarp and held a skin in his hands, something sloshed within. He looked to Bharath and stilled, craning his helmed gaze past him. Bharath cocked a brow, turned, and found the old man on all fours, lapping at the acrid toxicity like a starved dog. Guttural noises bellowed from deep in his throat. His eyes shot to Bharath, and they glowed.

Bharath clenched his eyes, reopened them, and saw the old man standing by his mule, whispering to his family again. Bharath swayed, and at the sound of shifting armor behind him, turned around. The Fetcher forced the skin and meat into his arms, then bent to retrieve the bartered weapon.

I'm getting worse, Bharath thought, and as he loaded the mule he glimpsed the Fetcher carve something in the salt with the butt of the gun. One word: ***LIAR.***

The Road

T he cool night looked down on them as they passed the Fetcher's wine across the fire, they and their mounts blemishes amidst the sprawling white. Having watered the mules, Bharath sat against his pack, rifle at his side, and gulped down another swig from the skin.

Good as ever, perhaps better, he thought, and in his drunkenness, stared at the one across from him. The mourner stared back, he and his sunken eyes dancing in the firelight. His gaze fell to the skin in Bharath's hands.

He has a taste for it, though he can hardly keep it down. Bharath passed the skin to the old man and his outstretched hands across the fire again, then tore a piece of roasted Brine in two, bringing one to his mouth. It tasted of salt, but of course it did. The old man pulled from the skin, convulsing as the liquid swam down his throat. He rocked once, twice, and brought the skin low again, wiping his mouth with his sleeve. He held it back to Bharath, who looked in the old one's eyes—eyes which didn't glow but when the flames caught them right, as any's would.

Bharath drank again, and the Brine burned on its way down. It seemed *different*, more potent than usual. Had the Fetcher perhaps changed a perfect concoction? He met the old man's sentry-gaze, saw the roasted meat at his feet untouched.

"Best eat," Bharath said, pulling the skin from his lips. "It doesn't keep, and there's barely enough for us." The old man's eyes fell to the wine again, and Bharath chuckled, handing it over. The mules laid still and sleeping, though one stared off in the middle-distance, pointed ears twitching, seemingly unbothered by the cumbersome weight of the dead still across its back.

Bharath leaned against his pack, glimpsing the mourner drinking again, and tilted his eyes to those magnificent stars. Fickle, uncaring gods; voyeurs, and twinkling sadists.

And he saw himself then, that first morning after they'd drugged and brought him to their tower. Stripped of everything but the memory of his failure, and what they'd told him before he awoke. That he was their ward, and would watch the southernmost side of their territory. He had earned this, they'd said, in their hooded robes. The Brine and stone in agreement on this manner of redemption. How he awoke shivering there, despite the heat sifting through the windowless pane. How the previous tenant, the skeleton in rags leaning against the stones, had smiled at him then, the rifle and boxes of ammunition beside him. How they'd welcomed Bharath to his new home.

"And they know what they do," Bharath said to them, staring down from their celestial plane, his words slurred. "Requiring you to come to *theirs* for sustenance. The Fetchers, who portion out meat every second day, and barely enough to get you through. See, Brine doesn't keep, despite the salt, and there's no stockpiling it...so eat up." Bharath drank from the skin, tears in his eyes. "I refused until my stomach fed upon itself, until Sarai whisp—"

"Like the old company towns in West Virginia," the old man said, his voice sweet on the air. Younger than his face portrayed. A rippling swam amidst the ether then, an expanding pressure. "Some things never change. Men are, *predictable...*"

"West Virginia?" Bharath asked, looking down from those stars to the mourner across the flames.

The mourner sighed, shook his head. "It's impossible to talk to you people, you know?" "World turns to ash, and you forget who you were."

The old man choked more of the wine down, dribbling some to the salt beneath him. He extended the skin back to Bharath, who took it in kind.

Mad fool, Bharath thought, and tipped it to his lips. This skin which never seemed to empty.

"You," Bharath said, doubt cast aside and gesturing to the mourner with the skin. "They will indoctrinate." He pulled a second time on the wine, the drink more potent than before, searing even. A mule snorted in the night, and the flatlands lie still. "Though if you refuse, and outlast the stone as I, you might gain tenancy of a tower when we return."

Bharath leaned forward. *We could turn back,* he thought. *Get the Fetcher to see reason. The three of us fortified in the tower might stand a chance, twenty zealots or no.*

"Where will we bury them?" he continued, looking to the bodies atop the mule behind the mourner.

"Wendover," the old man replied.

Bharath's eyes widened. "My grandfather said that's where they dropped it...a lifetime ago. What could possibly be there?"

The old man smiled, and the caverns in his face deepened. "That is the place. What more do you require?"

"Nothing." Bharath pulled on the wine again, heard the mourner's voice in his mind.

"They dropped them everywhere..."

How his gaze fell on Bharath like collapsed gravity.

"Hallelujah," the old man said with a smirk.

"What...?" Bharath slurred. Immobility seizing him as one of the two old man stretched the lids of his eyes wide, examining them.

The other smiled from across the fire. "An old saying..."

"You're nearly there. The first in recent memory, and my memory is long."

The world rocked beneath Bharath in a slow current, and he saw the mourner in doubled-image. The first drank from the skin again, still struggling to keep the potent drink down. The second stared into Bharath, his eyes glowing in the night, his thin lips around the wine skin, cheeks full and throat convulsing. The hide drenched in black, bubbling goop. It flowed from the old man's throat, his lips, into the skin's opening.

The old man coughed, retched, and Bharath shut his eyes, shook his head, reopening them. The mules turned his way now, and their eyes glowed.

Bharath stood, though he didn't remember doing so, and swayed on unsteady feet. The flames crawled higher, a many limbed thing which licked at the air. The old man rippled, distorted in Bharath's view, eyes still glowing.

Bharath saw her in his periphery on the edge of the camp where the light was faintest, lying in that sickbed. The black running from her eyes and lips. How he'd willed her to see that the Brine wasn't helping, wasn't a cure. That the Pillar, their shamans, knew nothing of the illness swept through the settlement. That their faith in the Brine and its potential for healing, wasn't hope, but death. That she was faithful, and that despite how faithful one might be, despite what the Pillar taught, the Brine cured none of anything.

The old man's visage swayed beyond the flame, and the night grew bright atop the salt flats surrounding them. He stood, and black liquid ran from his mouth down the front of his robes. "I'm told you lay with an irradiated stone for days. Death nor madness touching you."

Bharath smelled the metallic burning then. How in that week, the stone had become his god. How they'd thrown him and Kamber in separate cells when they'd failed to liberate Sarai. How they'd left him to rot twice as long as Sarai's blood relative.

Memory rolled atop reality as Bharath's vision swam through the night. How the old man crouched over the flames on hands and knees in the dark, black spurting from his mouth as he sucked in air. The two bodies strapped atop the mule sat up, they and their cloth-covered heads turning to Bharath.

And where there was no one, the mourner stood, his mouth to one of the dead one's throat. How the upright figure convulsed, as the old one drank them in with yellowed fangs. He turned to Bharath, and Bharath felt the weight of the skin in his hands, heavier than before, found himself knelt beneath the old man who was not an old man at all. The mules and his family looking down at him.

The mourner cupped Bharath's face, and the wind assaulted the flames, nearly extinguishing them. "When my family is reborn," he said, caressing Bharath's cheek with a lengthening thumb, "we might help you."

The mourner pointed to the skin by Bharath's slumped form, leaning against his leg. "*Driiink*," he cooed. "*Driiink*, child. You're nearly there."

Bharath nodded, and when he brought it to his lips, Sarai whispered what the Fetcher may never have carved in the lake's bank.

"*LIAR.*"

When Bharath pulled on the skin, he looked up at the mourner now turned away, his teeth sunk deep into the cloth-laden throat of the larger corpse. The mule's gaze still on him. Bharath groaned, dropped the hide to the salt, and touching his lips to his fingers, drew back a blackened liquid. The old man rose from the corpse, and it slumped there across the mule again. As he turned to Bharath, still kneeling there before him, he smiled, said words Bharath barely heard as his stomach wrenched with a hunger unknown—his tongue and teeth longing for the corpse above him.

"Soon, child," the voice said in his mind. The mourner taller than ever before. *"And here I was, of a mind to devour you."*

Bharath fell, and as the void rushed to meet him, he jolted upward, sucked in the air as if for the first time. His hands on the reins of his mule already at a steady trot. The old man a mule's length ahead, a risen hand gestured to the gleaming, fish-eye sun above. The mountains closer than ever, rising in the distance. A leviathan emerging from un-molested depths.

Bharath's heart pulsed in his ears as if submerged, the pounding spinning nausea in his gut and raw throat. He watched the mourner through a distorted haze.

The mourner gestured to the pass ahead, a jagged, open maw enticing them in, and then to the sky as the salt gave way to the intermingling clay. More patchwork tan working itself in amongst the white as they approached the rising peaks. He glanced back to Bharath, pointing to the sky, lips working, though producing no sound.

Bharath flexed his jaw wide, clearing his ears, but the pressure between the walls of his skull held firm. He lifted his chin, his head a hundred pounds, and his eyes latched to the reverberating image of the mourner still talking. Bharath wiped the spittle from his cracked lips, craned his head to listen.

"—a time when I could hardly look at it." The mourner dropped the reins of his mule, spread his arms wide, basked there in the sunlight. "Couldn't stand it whatsoever. How things have changed…"

Bharath thought the mourner looked younger now, the cavern-esque lines and divots risen some, the brows once white, now peppered black. How he sat tall, having filled out his robe, more muscular in his arms and legs as well.

"You're young…" Bharath said, or at least thought he did, and swayed there atop his mule, gripping the reins as

111

he watched a passing ridge, heard the voice again in his mind. *"I appear meek when it serves me."*

A sensation of floating overtook Bharath, and he lurched forward again, stomach plummeting. The ridge far behind them now. Bharath's skin audibly bubbled. The sun scalding his back and neck, and turning in his saddle, he saw the mule bearing their supplies tethered to his own. Its head bobbing with its steps, eyes gray, lifeless.

Bharath shook his head, coughed, and swung forward, bouncing with his mule's pace. The mourner and his mule faced him now, though they walked in reverse.

"Was a time I might look in someone's eyes and pull wires," the mourner said. "Make them see my way." Their mules snout to snout now, and as the old man spoke, he looked to the sun again.

"In the barrage, aspects were traded for others." He smiled, closed his eyes for the sun's gaze. "I feel it now, you know? Warmth..."

"I'm—" Bharath swayed on his mule, wrought with nausea. "I'm seeing things...hearing—"

The mourner trotted up beside Bharath, he and his mule still opposite his own. "Your man talked much on the trek to your tower."

"Unfriend, traitor..." Bharath groaned, and his vision grew hazy.

The mourner smiled. "Of your cell, your love..."

His voice softened, and Bharath peered ahead to the bronze-skinned woman in their path, dark hair rippling in the shadow of the ravine. Dark rivulets in lines from her nose and lips. Her eyes voids—ink-black.

Bharath lifted a hand to her, his throat raw, lungs burning, said, "Love…"

Sarai's head rose. The sun shimmering on the slab-stone cliffs. She seemed to float where the crest of the path met the horizon. The day's heat alchemizing the air in distorting waves. The salt-debris spiraling around her emaciated form. She rose her thin fingers, and though far in the distance, Bharath felt her caress on his face, closed his eyes, inhaled her plague breath.

"Life can't be all salt or sugar, love," she said, had said, was saying. "Its mixture, that's what gives life worth."

Her finger strummed Bharath's lips with its departure, and he fell into his saddle's frame, chasing her touch, eyes heavy now, though still upon her. If allowed, he would rot there, gazing on her till death swept him away because loneliness was a fate worse than hell. A fate Bharath had glimpsed, tasted—had no use for.

Sarai smiled as she fell, and what salt was there in the pass swarmed up over her. Miniature Brine coating her form until her bulk sank deep into the earth, deflating like a pierced lung.

"Look around, love," Bharath said. "Life's all salt without you here."

The sky was gray, though Bharath knew not when it had changed, and towering rock-face encroached on them from all sides, bent and peering upon their shuffling forms. They no more than the Brine which consumed Sarai. Bharath couldn't feel his legs, and he released the reins, gravity coaxing him backward.

"I have to stop…" he said, and slid from his mule to the ground. Slumped there on his back, he lay looking at an amorphous, darkening sky. Gathering vultures circling above. Bharath thought someone approached, though he couldn't be sure. For all he knew, he could be wandering the salt alone, could be sitting with the old man at the campfire, still passing the skin to and fro. He half-remembered strapping their gear to the mules this morning, kissing the fishbelly clavicle of one of the corpses before they'd embarked.

The mourner's face eclipsed the sky, peering down at Bharath, unblinking. His long black hair hung low.

"I'm dying…" Bharath said, and swallowing, he thought of the Pillar alive, well. Of Sarai, contorted and broken under their watch. Long gone from this plane, hoped he'd see her soon.

The mourner's lips drew taut, and he bent to Bharath, eyes glowing. He pried Bharath's lazy lids open, examined the eyes one at a time. His smile grew wide. "What is death but a parlor trick to one who may never die?"

Bharath averted his eyes from the mourner and those many teeth like the beaks of the demons swarming above. Their preened feathers floating down like ash, laying around Bharath in the dirt of the valley. Sarai knelt above him now, hand on his face. She kissed him then, and weak as he was, Bharath kissed her back. He placed his hands to her neck, felt something scramble up her throat, tepid and wriggling it broke from her lips, breached his own.

He gagged, gripped her hair in his fingers, and when he went to pull free, she held his mouth to hers with ease. He felt warmth slide out from the corner of his lips, and he gathered it with his tongue, swallowed it down. The iron taste forcing a smile from him.

"We're not all collars and capes anymore," the mourner said above him, wrapping a heft of cloth to his bleeding wrist. His somber gaze lost in the distance. "We're not much at all anymore…though we *will* be."

Bharath began to rise—found himself atop his mule. The landscape changed, transfigured. The mourner jerked the reins of his mule, which loosed a grunt from its flared nostrils. Bharath's stopped as well, shifting its head in the direction of the mourner's. The old man inhaled deep, and his spine popped with his arched back. The debris of the pass scattered with his echoing exhale.

"Wendover?" Bharath said, legs tingling with reanimated sensation. The pressure in his mind somewhat lessened.

The mourner glanced to Bharath, though his eyes remained down the pass. "No, child," he said, panting. He licked his lips. "Something else."

The Ruins

B harath took the scope from his eye and turned to the mourner crouching at the cliff's edge, overlooking the ruined structure below. A sprawling landscape of decrepit buildings, chunks torn and tossed aside by some colossus of a bygone age. The brick and concrete charred black, the sickly remnants of a makeshift barricade bent and twisted like a malformed spine. The vertebra torn asunder. Factions of stars impaling the night, the sky brimming lush with them.

Leaning forward, a growl rose in the mourner's throat, and as Bharath brought the scope to his eye again, he saw movement from the mouth of the largest structure. A sunken door tunneling into the face of the mountain itself. Faded symbols where the concrete met rock.

Figures clad in awkward, inflated suits emerged from the tunneling void, their wide-domed helmets and reflective face-shields obscuring their features. Bharath increased the magnification on his scope and saw the furthest figure from the entrance holding a yellow, box-like device in their hand. They lifted it to the others, and Bharath clocked the rifle the rearmost suit pulled, how they turned it on the one with the device, forcing the middle-most suit to move between them, their arms spread. Their muffled voices rose to the cliffs where Bharath and the mourner lay still. The one with the gun nudged the others back to the tunnel, and the one with the device held it up, shaking it while their free hand moved with their indecipherable words. The one with the rifle pulled it tight to their shoulder, and the one with the device threw up their hands in defeat as the three made for the tunnel again, disappeared down its throat.

Bharath set his rifle beside him and turned to the mourner. Stars reflected in his black eyes, drool from his lips to his chin, and his fingers unfurled, growing into ragged talons.

"LIAR," a voice rang, and Bharath jerked to its origin. Sarai looked down on him, her eyes pooled with plague. She shifted her gaze, and he followed it to the mourner who stood taller now, any semblance of that pained hunch a hazy memory. His eyes glowed like bullets near flame, and he turned to Bharath, touched a dirt-worn claw to the bandage at his wrist, then paused.

"I need my strength," he said. "After all, there are three, and it's been a *long* time. You'll manage, child."

Bharath groaned, wrapping his arms around himself.

The mourner leaned down, his eyes smoldering like doused embers. "Rest here a bit, hmm? Gather yourself as I"—he smirked—"parlay. Come once you've found your bearings, child. I know what it's like. Well…I remember."

Bharath couldn't move as he watched the mourner leap from the ledge, arms spread. He braced for the mourner's impact on the jagged rocks—heard nothing.

"What is happening to me?" Bharath whispered to the cool wind.

"Liar," it whispered back. The mules and their dead eyes piercing him.

He'd watched her there, as the Pillar's shamans drenched his love in the blood of the Brine, that holiest of creatures sprung forth from the salt lake. These dead and malleable gods. They bathed her, and all the afflicted, in the god-creature's blood. And the Pillar, quarantined and far from the plague's grasp, preached of life thereafter for the dying ones, those loyal to the Brine and its purpose to the end.

He remembered bursting through the door with Kamber, scavenged metal pipes in hand. How they'd held up the shamans before the zealots took hold of them, dragging them from the chamber as Sarai screamed, her tears black, blood from her raw voice misting the air. She lay contorted and bent as they took him from her. Threw he and Kamber in those dank cells, that whispering stone.

It had spoken to Bharath on that wet cell's floor. And he had eventually—between spurts of flaking flesh, bloodied skin, and distorted visions—spoken back. The stone had shown him his childhood home, Sarai, Kamber, the Pillar, and a hulking, albino Brine with translucent eyes crowding the cell's corner. Its pincers clutched as clasped hands. It was about to speak, when the zealots ripped him from the cage. Deemed him worthy of the Brine, despite his hatred and slight against them. Despite his desire to kill them all. They had escorted him to the tower, gave him a weapon, and in his rebellion, made him subservient. How Sarai screamed as she watched him pulled from her. How Bharath thrashed, an infant in their many-limbed grasp. How Sarai wailed the last time he saw his love alive.

Bharath opened his eyes and detached his teeth from the corpse strewn along the mule's back. He wiped his mouth, breath held as he collapsed, wide eyes staring at the pale arm draped from beneath the cloth covering, coaxing him nearer.

He heard screams and shambled to his feet, stronger now, coherent. He took up his rifle and made his way down the path, resisting the urge to satiate the corpses' call, willing him back to feed. He licked his lips—savored the taste—and pushing a loose tooth from his gums, ran his tongue over the bud of something new. Something sharp.

The peaks towered around him when he reached their base. The charred remains of the collapsed chain-link easily overstepped. Bharath held his rifle at the ready and kept low, skirting the downed semi-walls and punctured roofs. Strategically placing his footfalls in his approach to the makeshift camp.

He crouched behind a mound of fallen rubble, sniffed the air—how *rich* it was: the ash, the salt, an acidic tang intermingled there—and wrapped the strap of his rifle around his wrist. The tunnel before him an enormous, gaping maw. A prostrate leviathan who had only to shut its eyes to lure curious prey.

A sound tore through the tunnel, and Bharath craned his ear. A long, desperate scream. He nestled the rifle's barrel in the crook of the rubble. The cry bellowed again, followed by the patter of small arms fire. Bharath slowed his breathing, and all at once grew cold, as if someone watched him from afar. He lifted his gaze to the night sky, to the jagged peaks surrounding the remnants of…whatever this place was.

"Come," a voice in his mind said, and he straightened. It spoke again. *"Come."*

Bharath dropped the rifle and fell to the ground, clutching his head. Knees to his stomach and whimpering, he rocked back and forth, full well knowing the stone's influence was deep in his mind, guts, and bones now.

"Come," the voice spoke again, and chills swam through Bharath's entirety, forcing him upward. He took up his rifle and walked, compelled by the voice, though he didn't know why. And though he shook with each step, his blood was a torrent alive with the call—one he knew he must answer.

Hushed voices crawled throughout the funneled dark as Bharath held his rifle to his shoulder. The corridor was never-ending, and he found himself stumbling with the steady declination of the ground beneath him. He ventured further, weight shifted to his heels as the slope's slant increased. He figured it would be darker in the bowels of the mountain, given the light's absence, but he saw fine.

Should you be here? Sarai asked from beside him. Her eyes running black, those full lips a tight line. He held a hand to her, his eyes still down the rifle. She took it in her own, pressed his fingers to her lips.

They continued on, the hushed, sharp voices growing in clarity, and as the floor began to level, a doorway stood ahead. Beams of light pierced the dark in pointed arcs, swiveling from within the space beyond the entrance.

Bharath hugged the rightmost wall and trained his rifle on the strobing entrance. He turned to Sarai—no longer there—and the echoing voices drew his attention.

"Keep that rifle up," one said. "It's still here…"

"We need to leave, *now*," a raspy, deep voice. "Talia's hurt bad…and what the *hell was* that thing? We should never have come back, not without telling the others."

The scraping of boots along the ground, disturbing debris. "Says the one who *forced* us, said it *couldn't wait*. Besides, who knows if they're still there? They set up camp awful close to those crazies across the salt."

"Stop, both of you," a lighter voice said through labored breaths. "Stay alert. The breach has to be dealt with, yes, but we need to get out of here *alive* first."

Bharath rose. The stock of his rifle scraping a fastened pipe on the wall behind him.

"Oh, god." The deep voice again atop shuffling feet. "Oh god, it's outside."

Someone racked a shotgun. The *chk-chk* an unmistakably, universal language.

Bharath held his breath, and repositioned himself along the wall, his rifle trained on the open entrance. "Someone hurt in there?"

The voices spoke in muffled whispers, lined with the occasional squeal. Bharath heard rapid breaths, heartbeats pulsing in off-time rhythm within his skull.

"One of ours is injured," the deep voice said, and one of the others whispered something cut short. The deep voice continued. "It's not safe. There's something in here. Is your suit in good function?"

Bharath looked at the bare skin of his forearms, the dirty shirt and cuirass he wore—the rolled-up sleeves, his weathered boots. "Come on out. The entrance isn't far."

The voices dove in hushed tones. A mechanical crackling atop the low murmurs.

Bharath couldn't make out much:

Bait.

Door.

Trapped.

The deep voice rose. "You come to us."

Bharath grit his teeth, knowing a trap when he heard one, and turned to Sarai, inches from her now. Darkness running down her face.

"Don't abandon them, love," she said. "Not like me."

Bharath's lip trembled. "I'm so, so sorry…"

"What was that?" the voice asked again. "You coming in?"

"Come," the voice of his mind said, a rasp and in whispers. *"Through the doorway."*

Sarai nodded and, hand on Bharath's back, ushered him forward.

"Are you there?" the lighter voice said, weaker than before.

"I'm coming in," Bharath said. "Don't think me naive. Understand?"

"Yes, just hurry. Please."

Bharath stuck the barrel through the entrance first and slowly crept inside. The space opened wide into a dome with high walls, metal and concrete lining the ceiling above. Doorways lay in a semi-circle to the rear of the three at the room's center. Their suits gleamed silver, concealing their forms, and face-shields reflected what little light shone from their headlamps.

The figure with the shotgun gasped. "You don't have a suit. How are you…?"

One of them crouched over the other who sat holding their side, and turned to Bharath, lifting a yellow, crackling device via metal handle, which squealed and popped more violently as the silver suit extended it Bharath's way.

Bharath cleared his throat, his rifle steady. "It's safe, *clean*. Look." He inhaled deep.

The figures looked to one another, the beams of their headlamps slicing through the low-light, and as the one with the crackling machine nodded, the other trained the shotgun on Bharath.

"Hey now, hold on." Bharath said, eyeing them each in turn.

"Your eyes…you can see down here?" the one with the device said, head tilting from their static machine to Bharath.

"Drop the rifle," the wounded suit said. Bharath noticed her face shield was cracked. The others fanned off from their wounded in opposite directions. A flank in the making.

"She said drop it," said the one with the shotgun. The weapon's silent mouth open, dialed in on Bharath as the pair drew closer.

Can I make the door? Bharath thought. Knew he couldn't.

The voice in his mind spoke. *"Fear serves them well, but it won't save them…"*

A shroud swooped from the ceiling, crumpling the figure with the gun in a series of bone-snapping crunches. The weapon sailed from their hands. Their gurgled groan cut short by Bharath's shot from his hip at the one with the device. Their dropped machine crackled, whining there in piercing agony as its wielder did much the same. Blood welled from their abdomen as their chest rose and fell, enveloping the silver in crimson.

A tall figure stood between Bharath and the injured woman, who slid back against the wall.

"See, child?" the mourner asked, still facing the wheezing woman. *"This* is how they should look at us. How they *once looked* at us. How they feared to speak our names, *hint* at our existence."

The woman screamed and swung her arm upward, too quick to clock. Two flashes illuminated the room, sending echoes throughout the tunnel. The mourner jerked in time with them, though otherwise remained stalwart. He growled and strode towards the pleading woman, the click of the revolver the only sound before he punched through her suit, grabbing her by the throat. Her feet kicked for purchase, as if treading a soul starved sea.

"Was a time when they sought me out..." the mourner said, the woman clawing at his outstretched arm. He seemed unbothered by her flailing. "Some to kill, but every now and then, to *become*." The mourner glanced at him now, and Bharath only recognized him for his voice. His widened mouth full of sharp, yellowed teeth. His slanted eyes gleaming like a cat's in shadow.

The woman kicked at the mourner's hip, and he shook her, throttling her against the wall with a *thwack*. Something popped in the violence, and she fell still, whimpering in his grasp. The one Bharath had shot groaned on the concrete, gloved hands clutching their stomach for all the blood seeping out.

Bharath lifted his rifle on the mourner, and the tall thing chuckled. "See how they tremble, child? How her eyes absorb what she cannot comprehend? What her entirety *longs* to deny? What they all unknowingly wish so desperately died with their world?"

Bharath backed to the door, loaded another round. "I'm not like you. Whatever you are."

"No?" the mourner asked with a smile, teeth jutting in a dozen directions. "Whether you choose it or not, you will see things my way. Observe."

The mourner lowered the woman, her boots brushing the floor now, and the nails on his free hand grew hooked, taloned. He sliced a line in his wrist through the bandage, and blood fell to the earth, sizzling, hissing. Bharath felt the urge to charge then, to latch onto the exposed wrist. He shook before he fell to the ground, resisting with all he was left, his body screamed for the blood, as the yellow machine whined more than ever before. The two suits on the ground convulsed now, limbs sporadic as they gagged, writhing, hands clawing at their face-shields, and soon the pair's flailing lessened, died.

Poison, Bharath thought, from somewhere deep within himself, though he crawled on hands and knees for the loosed blood, mouth gaping, tongue lolling. His gums bled, aflame with pain as he spat the remainder of his teeth.

"Are you not like me?" the mourner said in his mind. *"Set apart?"*

The mourner peered into the woman's eyes, holding his bleeding wrist to her. She turned her head away, feet scraping the ground now and again. *"Look. Resilient, resistant—like you."*

The woman went for something at her belt, but the tall one was fast. He thrust her head to the wall and it rocked with a thump. She slackened then, and the mourner brought her limp form close. Bharath's mouth watered at the blood still hissing beneath him.

The mourner tilted her chin and jerked his head forward—once, twice—and a blackened sludge hung there a moment, his open lips inches from her own. The black twitched, clawing for her lips, and sank in a slow crawl into her open mouth. She struggled, and he shook her till she swallowed it down. The mourner's eyes rolled back and he eased her to the floor, hand cradling her head as he propped her against the wall. She lolled, her chest rising and falling in an off-kilter rhythm. The mourner wiped the excess from the corner of her lips.

"What…are you?" Bharath slurred through the hungry drool of a toothless mouth. The pangs in his gut electric, eyes bulging.

The mourner smiled with a mouth of razors. "What am I? Well…I'm home. *We're home.*"

The lines of his face rippled then, as if something inchoate swam just beneath the skin.

Bharath moaned as he latched to the tall one's wrist, and before his eyes rolled with ecstasy, he glimpsed Sarai at the doorway licking her lips.

The Decree

D arkness, save for the flickering beam of the corpse's headlamp. Save Sarai's face near his own. She ran a hand through his hair, smiled as black liquid bubbled between her teeth.

Why, Bharath thought, as she caressed his cheek with her thumb. *Why must I remember you like this? As you were, at the end. Why not the jovial woman I strode the salt with, in search of better things?*

Bharath shook his head as the tears came. *No…this is what I deserve, but not you, never you…*

She—eyes twin, glistening voids—smiled then, kissed him. Bharath swallowed the warmth she expelled. She withdrew from him, and a string of oily drool connected their moist lips.

How the scourge burned within his throat, and though he fought to keep it down, he *craved* it, had come to *need* it. He looked into her eyes. "Are you here at all, love? Or am I just telling the story of me to myself?"

Across the dome room, the woman, silver suit peeled from her, moaned, dried blood in crimson down her face and chin. Her breath was rapid now, and she twitched, kicking in spurts, her eyes on the ones she once knew, still motionless.

Bharath looked at the words along the top of the doorway ahead of him. The concrete shown brighter where someone tall had wiped it away.

—GEOLOGIC REPOSITORY—
—CAUTION: RADIOACTIVE MATERIALS—

A tingling between his shoulders stilled him.

"Come."

He rose to his feet, adjusting his cuirass, bent to retrieve his rifle.

"Leave it, child." The voice a whisper on the stagnant air.

Bharath held his hand there, suspended. The rifle was an extension of himself, or at least, it had been. He pulled his hand away, leaving the weapon to rest in the rubble.

The woman shifted as Bharath neared the door and he met her bloodshot, luminescent eyes.

She coughed and cleared her throat. "Your eyes," she whispered. "What *are* you...?"

Bharath looked into her own and didn't have it in him to tell her that whatever *he was, she* was, too.

"Liar," he said, before heading to the doorway beside her. Across the way's opening in blackened, bold letters read:

THIS PLACE IS NOT A PLACE OF HONOR. NO HIGHLY ESTEEMED DEED IS COMMEMORATED HERE. NOTHING VALUED IS HERE.

The floor slanted downward, and every few strides, Bharath found more text emblazoned above on horizontal slabs of protruding stone.

WHAT IS HERE WAS DANGEROUS AND REPULSIVE TO US.

A tingling on his arms, the back of his neck. A metallic tang in the air growing warm.

THE DANGER IS IN A PARTICULAR LOCATION. IT INCREASES TOWARDS THE CENTER. THE CENTER OF DANGER IS HERE, OF A PARTICULAR SIZE AND SHAPE, AND BELOW US. THE DANGER IS STILL PRESENT, IN YOUR TIME, AS IT WAS IN OURS.

Sarai walked with him now, clutched his hand as they descended deeper into the earth.

THE DANGER IS TO THE BODY, AND IT CAN KILL.

THE FORM OF THE DANGER IS AN EMANATION OF ENERGY.

THE DANGER IS UNLEASHED ONLY IF YOU SUBSTANTIALLY DISTURB THIS PLACE PHYSICALLY.

Two enormous, cracked metal doors stood before him, and if not for their girth and the indentations of monstrous hands bending the metal of each inward, they might've seemed impenetrable. They were ajar, a sliver of darkness the width of a person at their center. Metal bolts and hinges were wrenched out from the top and bottom of the behemoths, and Bharath peered at the last of the text.

THIS PLACE IS BEST SHUNNED AND LEFT UNINHABITED.

"Come, child," the mourner said from within, and Bharath sidestepped through the narrow opening. Two gleaming orbs pierced the dark, and the mourner sprawled amidst a wrecked formation of yellow, cylindrical containers bearing the same insignia as the doorway in the dome, **RADIOACTIVE** stamped across each.

133

The grouping of cannisters nearest the mourner sliced open and torn apart, an ash like layered, colored glass from corroded radiation covered him. He laid there, on his back, basking in what the cylinders once held.

"Do your new eyes serve you well?"

Bharath placed a hand on a nearby drum, legs grown weak.

"I thought you might have known," the mourner said, eyes still gleaming in the dark. "At your tower, when you didn't *invite me in*..." He smiled and stood in the hazardous mess wrought from the barrels. They receded in stacked rows as far as Bharath could see.

Bharath released the barrel, swaying, but managed to stand on his own. "Is this...are we to bury them here?"

The mourner smiled and observed the ceiling, chin in his hand.

"Who, child?"

Bharath grew numb, his heart *thump-thumping* in his ears. He longed for his rifle. "Your *family*, the ones strapped to that mule."

The mourner chuckled, his bare feet in wet slapping echoes along the earth as he paced. "Oh, I've been lying to your kind since before the world died. They are of no more use to me than the skin holding your wine."

Bharath wondered if he could clear the tomb before the mourner took him down, doubted it.

"This world," the mourner said, arms spread over the subterranean, "has been reborn, though it's no longer theirs. Too long have we lived with them in secret. *Now* the world is clay, putty *we* will mold. They will throw down their false *gods*, their doctrine glorifying a mutation no smarter than when it was the size of a fingernail. They shall one by one be tested. Be as we are, or husks for our purpose." The mourner lifted a finger to Bharath. "You will go to those in the settlement. You, my messenger, my prophet. Bring them this message, child, and return with those of a propensity to become."

"I," Bharath began. "I don't understand…You'd save those who took my love from me?"

"We'd save all we can," the mourner said, and the sound of bare feet pattering on the concrete behind Bharath forced him to turn. The woman stood, her eyes glowing in the dim light. The mourner turned up his palm and she cocked her head upward, as if hearing a voice Bharath did not. She padded past him to the mourner, her gait unsteady as she took his hand. "All who possess the means to be born again."

The mourner cupped the woman's face, and she nuzzled into his touch. "We're building a world, too, child. They in the settlement may be the beginnings of the dream of my family, as are you—the hope that we rise again."

"I don't understand…" Bharath said again, and he felt the shame build with the words though he could not say why. "What are you…? What am I?"

"Oh, child," the mourner said. "That is the question, isn't it? What are we *now*, in this irradiated world? I don't think it's so much the blood anymore, but what lies *within*. The tinge, the poison. See, we are a new creature, Bharath, though now, like you, even *I* am become something new."

The mourner bit into his wrist, and let the blood fall to the ash, it hissed there, churning the powder to a thick liquid. The woman fell to her knees, lapping the newness with her tongue. She slid forward as it coagulated, as it rose around her and the mourner's feet. She rolled on her back, smiling, her breath low and full. She ran her arms and legs in the muck, and as the mourner spread his arms wide, his eyes turned milky.

Bharath's words came in spurts. "And if…I were to do this…if I were to go back—"

A smile broadened across the mourner's face, and the woman sat upright from her position in the liquid waste. Barrels burst around them with the sludge's caress.

"Look," she said, her yellow eyes on Bharath as she swayed, and though she formed the words, Bharath sensed it was the mourner. "How he still speaks in terms of *if* and *but*… You have died, child, have been reborn a new creature. *Thrall* is the old word, and as such, you are *mine*."

The mourner affixed himself to the concrete via the now glowing sludge, and his flesh tore free from the earth as he walked to Bharath, groaning in pain.

"This is how we live again," he said as the woman laid down, running her hands and legs under the fresh toxicity. "We are linked, you and I, and there is *nowhere* you might go I cannot find you."

The mourner's lips drew taut, and his voice rose in Bharath's mind. *"Betray me, Thrall, and I will speak till you go mad, till you beg for your former sickness. I have bestowed on you this greatest of gifts. You are mine."*

The mourner cupped Bharath's cheek, and a euphoria flooded him… his wants… thoughts of revenge… fears… all melted away by the quiet calm of the mourner's touch. He withdrew his hand from Bharath, who lurched before collapsing.

He looked up at the mourner through tears, longing for the glimpsed peace. The woman's eyes still rolled back in utter ecstasy. Envy pooled in Bharath's gut, grew frigid there.

"My child," the mourner said, a metallic tang emanating off him. "Cast aside your old life…none die who are worthy. Understand?"

Bharath hesitated, and the mourner gripped his throat, holding him aloft with ease. The euphoria pulsed through Bharath in a maelstrom, and his lips formed a wide smile with his creator's words.

"It is not of the individual, but the many become one. I see that now…what I am. Test them, and bring them here. Let them serve you, as you serve me. I will see through your eyes, and I will be with you. Go now, gather my family. Bring them to me, so we may be as one."

The mourner released him, and as Bharath turned for the gap in the doors and the world above, he thought of an old fantasy. The Pillar, enslaved, and how laying them here at his master's feet would rob them of everything they were.

As he ascended, Bharath thought on how that might do Sarai justice—how it would *have* to—though the rot-scent of the dead in the dome forced the image asunder. Bharath's nostrils flared with the reek of their irradiated blood. The marrow still in their bones. His lips spread wide then, teeth grew long.

The Pillar

E ven as the zealots dismounted their mules—clad in golden-Brine armor and training their rifles on him—the Fetcher did not move. He sat at his workstation, armor-clad himself, because it was forbidden to shed it being of the Brine. An oath sworn when he was made Fetcher on the periphery of the dead lake.

The zealots' armor gleamed in the full, unrelenting sun, and if not for the shade of the Fetcher's helmet, he may have lifted a hand to see more clearly the three zealots walking towards him, broken off from the others still mounted. A full raiding party, no less than twenty mule-back, seething with bloodlust.

As the Fetcher adjusted his posture, the rightmost zealot's rifle jerked up. The centermost zealot—shorter, more lean, and wearing the hollowed skull of an adolescent Brine atop her head—raised her hand, stayed her comrade's weapon.

"Fetcher," she said, palm on the sawed-off shotgun at her hip, dark hair lifted from the breeze skidding atop the lake. The Fetcher's head imperceptibly rose, his eyes on hers beneath the thick of his salt-rusted helmet. "The heretic," she continued, "the one he was leading. Have they come?"

The zealot at her left scanned the lake, the one on the right glared holes through the Fetcher, finger still caressing his rifle's trigger.

The Fetcher shook his head, and looked to the black, steaming pool belching near the formation of the still-mounted party. The stench of sulfur ripe on the breeze, the air hung with it.

She sighed, her finger tapping the shotgun. "You're good, Fetcher. The very best. The helmet you crafted serves me well, but I, *as you*, serve the Brine. Seeing as the heretic's tower is abandoned, and you've no word regarding he or his quarry…" She straightened. "You are to be brought before the Pillar."

The Fetcher looked off at the lake, to the once-still waters disturbed by a thrashing Brine. Translucent pincers and jutting antennae leaping above where the water met the atmosphere. The rusted cage rocked below the water's surface, and though the chains squealed, they held.

"Speak, *Shrimper*," the rightmost zealot said, his rifle's gaze on the Fetcher again. "A high zealot addresses you."

Brine-helm placed her hand on the zealot's chest plate, and though larger than she, he stilled. The wind, peppered with grunting mules, kicked up salt from the bank in a maelstrom.

"A zealot," she began, the cloths before the shop's entrance whipping in the gust. "Any *good* zealot would know Fetchers' tongues are removed upon their swearing. Everything you are, you owe this one here."

She looked to the Fetcher again, whose slitted-helmet took them in. A being of utter stillness.

"His gesture was answer enough," she continued, motioning to one of the riders behind her. They trotted over, a long-tipped spear in their hands. "See how he stares at the violent almighty, the dead lake's offering? Even on the brink of his own destruction, the Fetcher thinks on his calling. Wholly mindful of the Brine until his days bleed out, that he might rest beneath the lake with them. But *you*…know little of our ways…have tested me this entire venture."

The rifleman straightened as the spear nestled in the crook beneath his helm, flush with his throat, the beating pulse therein.

The high zealot unsheathed her shotgun, and the leftmost zealot trained their rifle on the whimpering man whose own weapon fell to his feet. He cried out, as the Fetcher looked on, and the mounted one directed him with the spear in prodding nudges to the edge of the acrid pool nearby.

With the flick of the high zealot's wrist, the spearman thrust the outcast forward, the black of the pool hissing as it devoured him, his screaming cut short. The reek of seared flesh and burnt hair rose from the pit. When the turbulence calmed, became docile, the high zealot turned to the Fetcher.

"Rise," she said, and the Fetcher did. "Take up his mount."

The Fetcher stepped forward, and the zealot guard held their rifle at-ease, waiting behind the high zealot, whose dark hair whipped awry in the wind.

He walked within paces of the two Brine-soldiers, and stopped, glancing back to the Brine in its cage, maniacal at the serrated bars of its prison. The cage rocked beneath the frenzied waters. A hand fell on the Fetcher's shoulder, though he did not break his gaze from the Brine, from the great sword still impaled in the earth near the pulley and crank.

"There will be another to complete the work," the high zealot said as her hand fell from his rusted pauldron. "Come, faithful, let's see this done."

The Fetcher turned, walked with the zealots to those mounted. The spearman led from atop his mule, flicking the blood from the outcast to the salt before sheathing it at his side. The crimson stark on the unblemished white.

The Fetcher glanced over his shoulder again, down the salt-laden coast, past the Brine, sword, and cage blurring into that distorting horizon, and thought that, if he squinted, he could see a lone mule draped in cloth.

Bells rang atop clanging poles as they entered the settlement, for those gone, those to go yet. They dismounted and splintered into parties, their armor glinting gold in the harsh sunlight.

How much of that armor was the Fetcher's own doing? he wondered, and caught glimpses of shivering townsfolk, young and old alike, dressed in rags and ruin in the alleys and dank crevices of the red-clay lean-tos they passed. So many crude shelters huddled together comprising the promise of life, one better than endlessly wandering beyond the settlement's walls.

Zealots fell in around him, but the Fetcher was lost in thought as the high zealot took up the front of the column. He saw himself in one of the shelters here not long ago. How that place had been filled with a moment's dream of peace, a future, before he had been called to act by morality's inconvenient compass. The clay and salt transfigured into older memories now. Of a boy, elsewhere beyond the mountain, not a grain of salt to be seen amongst the pale, leafless trees. A laugh bellowing deep from within his throat, a ferocious joy he would never know again.

The settlement opened into a makeshift square where more downtrodden stood outside an ashen-stone structure. Their bowed heads low as the zealots crossed their path. The high zealot stopped, and so did the Fetcher, the rest of them, their gaze climbing the array of salt-sprinkled steps to the lone figure in brown robes at the height of the stairs. The cloaked one held a clay urn in their hands. The silence grew as they stared up at the robed one, before the shaman turned, cloak whipping behind him.

The people lifted their hands then, and fell prostrate and mumbling, their lips pressed to the earth. The high zealot glanced over her shoulder, the Brine pauldron obscuring most of her face. "They pray for you," she said, and the Fetcher jerked at her voice. "As do we all." Palm on her shotgun, she ascended the steps, and the party followed her, the incessant groans of a stricken people ushering them on.

The room's interior was dark but for the openings in the ceiling, and atop the raised platform in the back of the interior sat five cloaked figures in Brine-shell chairs. The zealots at the party's rear remained by the barred wooden door, and only after the shaman poured Brine oil on the newcomers' hands and helms, were they allowed to approach the Pillar.

As the shaman replaced the urn with the others at the base of the platform, the second left of the Pillar clasped their hands, spoke. "What news of the heretic…?"

"None, Glory…" the high zealot said, removing her helm. "The ward's tower is abandoned, and there has not been word nor sight of them since their departure."

The cloaked ones mumbled among themselves, turned in on one another, and the Fetcher lifted his head to the enormous Brine edifice behind them. Its bulbous sockets swallowing him whole.

"This one must die," the rightmost Pillar said, a trembling finger marking the Fetcher.

The cloaked figures nodded to one another, and the Fetcher heard the zealots behind him, their armored plates sliding out from one another. The shaman walked behind the platform, and reemerged with a hollowed leg of manipulated Brine, gnarled and twisted. They placed it to their lips, blew.

An armored figure swept away the flowing cloth from the doorway by the platform, hefting a two-handed axe. He wore no helmet, and his olive skin shone in what sun the blemished ceiling allowed. He stood between the Pillar and the now condemned, his armor not Brine, but leather—a wanderer's garb. His face covered in dirt and ash, dusting his black beard.

"And how many heads have you brought, Kamber?" the centermost figure said, clasping his hands. "How many do you bestow today on you and your blood's behalf?"

"One of three, Glory," Kamber said, and turned to the high zealot, who began to whisper in the Fetcher's ear.

"Next you know, you'll join those gods below the dead lake's waters. A high honor." She placed a hand on the Fetcher's shoulder, held pressure there, and he knelt. Kamber raised the two-handed axe, the blade kissing the crook between the Fetcher's helm and rusted armor.

"For the Pillar, for the Brine," Kamber said above him. "In recompense, for me and mine. I pay the debt, a head at a time. In hope she's well there, in the light."

The Fetcher was still.

The leftmost Pillar member leaned forward. "And what have you to say in defense of your failure, Fetcher?"

"Glory," the high zealot said. "You know, as I, Fetchers' tongues are—"

A chair toppled to the floor. "*Silence, servant.* We speak to him as we would the heretic."

A voice from the opposite end of the platform now. "If he is innocent, let him speak."

The Fetcher heaved in air, and it bellowed against the metal of his helm in a deep echo. He pressed the skin of his neck to the axe head, slid it along the edge. Blood ran in thin rivulets to the earth, sizzling, bringing rise to wispy tendrils.

The axe rose from the Fetcher's skin, and Kamber fell backward, kicking and wheezing, clawing at his throat, eyes bulging as the two zealots at the door fell as well, convulsing and foaming at their mouths.

"Her name was Sarai," Bharath said, and stood as the high zealot, prostrate and writhing, vomited blood on his boot. She gripped his ankle, eyes pleading, and he kicked her away. His gaze gorging on the cloaked ones writhing and vomiting upon the platform, collapsing into chairs, desperately tearing at their robes as their god looked on from behind.

Kamber backed against the platform at Bharath's approach, knocking an urn to the earth, spilling Brine. The blood came up from his throat again, and he reached a weak hand for the axe Bharath now hefted, testing its weight. The Fetcher's helm cast to the floor in its place.

"Bha...Bharath," Kamber said, his voice raspy, barely audible for the violent convulsions of the Pillar above the platform. "How are...you're—"

Bharath glowered over his love's traitor-brother, lips taut. "Do you even hear Sarai anymore?"

Two Pillar members crawled along the floor and drew Bharath's gaze. Tears fell from their eyes, their hoods thrown back to reveal their less than god-like faces, vomiting less and less with each ragged cough. Bharath smiled.

"Bharath," Kamber said, his breath weakening, head lolling against the platform's base. "You're sick...your eyes...what have you done?"

Bharath looked down on him, opened his mouth to speak, but a faint voice in his mind interrupted.

"These, my child," it said from far away. *"These who do not wither under the weight of our blood. They are the stones with which we rebuild. I will give you the words, Thrall. Speak now, illuminate them to the world which awaits."*

Bharath tilted his head, caught the glint of the Fetcher's helm at his feet, still tasted the Shrimper's blood on his tongue. He'd given their servant ample time to consider rebellion, long before he'd torn him apart and fed him in pieces to the newly caged Brine caught just as he'd arrived.

Bharath turned to Kamber, whose eyes widened.

"What have you done, Bharath. What have you done...?"

The voice in his mind, hollow, and far off. *"Turn them, child."*

Bharath raised the axe over his head, and as Kamber and the mourner cried out, he brought it down again, again, again. The staccato rhythm of flesh, sinew, and bone vibrated through his arms as the weapon fulfilled its purpose. Bharath overstepped what was once Kamber, leaping with ease to the platform where the last Pillar member bent in on themselves, eyes clenched in agony. Screaming, rocking, eyes opening at the sound of Bharath's boots upon the structure. The cloaked one lifted a hand to the great Brine skeleton, bringing a smile to Bharath's lips. *What is worse?* Bharath thought. *To not know the lie for what it is, or to know and still desperately believe...?*

"*I command you, Thrall, spare him. You will obey.*"

A fear rose in Bharath then, some connection to the blood flowing within him, but he forced it aside, and knew that just as he had become something new, so had the mourner. How it pained his master to rise from the poison in the ruins. He had become weak, reliant.

The voice grew in ferocity, booming within the walls of his skull. "*Do you not wish for the paradise shown you?*"

Bharath fell to the platform, armor clanging. He rocked there, whimpering, blood boiling, until a hand gripped the nape of his neck. He placed his atop it, and looked up at Sarai smiling, her black eyes gleaming. Hers the only voice he cared to hear.

"*Shhhhhhhh,*" she said. "*Shhhhhhh...*"

"*It can still be yours, child,*" his master said again. "*I am forgiving, like any good father, of mistakes and slights against me, though you must obey.*"

Bharath remembered the euphoria of the mourner's touch. How nothing had mattered suspended in that near perfection. How Sarai quieted in the bliss of that pseudo-heaven. Bharath needed her more than some dead euphoria. The world had died twice, once in flames long

149

ago, and again when she was taken from him. He thought of the stone then, near now, still in that cell they'd thrown him. Thought of the albino Brine in the cage's corner, if it still had words for him, and if so, what it might say.

His master's voice rose in a swarm again, searing the blood in his veins, but Bharath spoke over it as Sarai squeezed his hand.

"See through my eyes, Master," he said, and rose to his feet, his hand in love's. "See how the blade cuts through them." He dragged the axe one-handed behind him, and a scream formed on the face of the last alive. "How it turns its gaze to you."

ABOUT THE AUTHORS

SCOTT J. MOSES is the author of *Non-Practicing Cultist* (Demain Publishing) and *Hunger Pangs* (independently published). A member of the Horror Writers Association, his work has appeared in *Paranormal Contact* (Cemetery Gates Media), *Diabolica Americana* (Keith Anthony Baird), *Planet Scumm*, and elsewhere. He also edited *What One Wouldn't Do: An Anthology on the Lengths One Might Go To*. He is Japanese American and lives in Baltimore. You can find him on Twitter @scottj_moses or at scottjmoses.com.

CARSON WINTER is an author, punker, and raw nerve. He's a minimalist weirdo, a conversational absurdist, and a vehemently bleak-minded artist making his home in the Pacific Northwest. You're looking for his words? You don't want those. But if you're going to insist, poke around the cold alleys of *Vastarien*, *Apex*, and *The No Sleep Podcast*. You want something longer? Okay, well, he also has a novella called Reunion Special. If that's not enough and you want more Carson Winter roiling in your stomach and mind, find him on Twitter @CarsonWinter3 or at carsonwinter.com. But please, be careful.

ABOUT THE ARTISTS

MARISA BRUNO is an American artist and illustrator who creates unsettling black and white drawings. She works primarily with an ordinary ballpoint pen, taking inspiration from legends, nightmares and the writing of authors like M.R. James and Clive Barker. Marisa makes horror at her home in Rochester, NY. Find her on Instagram @marisabrunoart and Twitter @marisashorror.

EVANGELINE GALLAGHER is an award-winning illustrator from Baltimore, Maryland. They received their BFA in Illustration from the Maryland Institute College of Art in 2018. When they aren't drawing they're probably hanging out with their dog, Charlie, or losing at a board game. They possess the speed and enthusiasm of 10,000 illustrators.